FATAL REUNION

A James Acton Thriller

Also by J. Robert Kennedy

James Acton Thrillers

The Protocol	Blood Relics	The Viking Deception
Brass Monkey	Sins of the Titanic	Keepers of the Lost Ark
Broken Dove	Saint Peter's Soldiers	The Tomb of Genghis Khan
The Templar's Relic	The Thirteenth Legion	The Manila Deception
Flags of Sin	Raging Sun	The Fourth Bible
The Arab Fall	Wages of Sin	Embassy of the Empire
The Circle of Eight	Wrath of the Gods	Armageddon
The Venice Code	The Templar's Revenge	No Good Deed
Pompeii's Ghosts	The Nazi's Engineer	The Last Soviet
Amazon Burning	Atlantis Lost	Lake of Bones
The Riddle	The Cylon Curse	Fatal Reunion

Special Agent Dylan Kane Thrillers

Rogue Operator	Black Widow	State Sanctioned
Containment Failure	The Agenda	Extraordinary Rendition
Cold Warriors	Retribution	Red Eagle
Death to America		The Messenger

Templar Detective Thrillers

The Templar Detective	The Sergeant's Secret	The Black Scourge
The Parisian Adulteress	The Unholy Exorcist	The Lost Children
	The Code Breaker	

Kriminalinspektor Wolfgang Vogel Mysteries

The Colonel's Wife	Sins of the Child

Delta Force Unleashed Thrillers

Payback	Kill Chain	The Cuban Incident
Infidels	Forgotten	Rampage
The Lazarus Moment		Inside the Wire

Detective Shakespeare Mysteries

Depraved Difference	Tick Tock	The Redeemer

Zander Varga, Vampire Detective

The Turned

FATAL REUNION

A James Acton Thriller

J. ROBERT KENNEDY

UnderMill PRESS

ISBN: 9781990418297

First Edition

For those murdered by the Russian Federation in Ukraine.

FATAL REUNION

A James Acton Thriller

"Family quarrels are bitter things. They don't go according to any rules. They're not like aches or wounds, they're more like splits in the skin that won't heal because there's not enough material."

Babylon Revisited
F. Scott Fitzgerald

"This is a very violent place to live, the Earth, and we're a very violent species. Cain is still killing Abel. We see that every day."

Anne Lamott

PREFACE

The Ayutthaya Kingdom ruled much of what is now modern-day Thailand for over 400 years, and was responsible for turning the region into a center of international trade with a flourishing culture. The kingdom made contact with European traders, and in 1686 sent a delegation to meet with the court of King Louis XIV of France.

King Borommakot reigned for 25 years, the period peaceful, with arts and culture thriving. He died leaving a robust kingdom with tremendous wealth and a powerful military that had fought off numerous invasion attempts by neighboring enemies.

The question is why, after over 400 years, did tradition fail, leading in just nine years to the collapse of the kingdom? All that is known is that there was a feud over who should succeed after Borommakot's death, for the coronation was anything but smooth.

As is so often true between royal brothers.

Thailand

Present Day

Retired British Special Air Service Lt. Colonel Cameron Leather raised his weapon, his finger slipping onto the trigger of his M4 assault rifle. But he stopped. The roar of agony from a man he respected tremendously demanded action, yet he couldn't interrupt what was unfolding before him.

For if he did, this man's sacrifice would be for naught.

The machete sliced across the man's chest a second time, the open wound visible even from this distance in the firelight, and the scrape of the blade suggested the gang leader had reached the ribcage. Another roar of agony, this time weaker, erupted, and thankfully the man he was supposed to protect passed out, temporarily ending his suffering.

The gang leader stepped back, his blade dripping in blood gripped in one hand, and the artifact this was all about in the other. So much death, so much suffering, all over something discovered by accident, lost centuries ago.

Yet would it buy his people a reprieve? The gang had been pursuing them for hours through the jungle, determined to slaughter every man, woman, and child. Motivated by revenge for an untimely, innocent death, as well as greed, they were determined to possess what this hero had just given them in an attempt to buy those he loved a chance.

Leather prayed the man remained unconscious, yet he wouldn't, for he was too strong, too stubborn, and knew the longer he stayed alive as a distraction, the more distance the people he was dying for could put between them and their pursuers.

Leather cursed as their potential savior stirred.

And Hugh Reading once again stared his captor in the eyes, ready to die for those he loved.

I swear you'll be avenged, my friend.

Ayutthaya, Ayutthaya Kingdom
April 25, 1758

Prince Uthumphon sprinted along the central road that cut through the capital city, his personal guard clearing a path while struggling to provide the protection he was due. But these were his people. He didn't fear them, nor they him. He occupied the luxurious position of second son. It meant he was an honored member of the royal family, and second in line to the throne by tradition, but his father had plenty of years left in him, and his elder brother many more beyond that.

It gave him the luxury of being friendly to their subjects, and he was loved for it. Yet today, the hordes wishing him well were in the way, delaying his urgent journey, spurred by a message he had received while supervising the bridge repair across the gorge that cut them off from their territory to the south. The old bridge had partially collapsed in the last monsoon season, and repairs were desperately needed, so he had been tasked to get it done by his father, King Borommakot.

It was an honor to have been given such an important undertaking, but the assignment had unfortunately widened the gulf that existed between him and his brother, Thammathibet. The job should have been given to his brother, but he was too unreliable. He was more concerned with food, drink, and women—the trappings of his position. And while Uthumphon enjoyed all three as well, he never let them get in the way of his duties.

He had excelled, of course, as he always did, and the bridge was nearing completion when the messenger arrived from the city informing him his father had fallen gravely ill.

And the long sprint home had begun.

He loved his father, and his father loved him. Perhaps a little too much, in that he clearly favored him over Thammathibet. Their mother had died while giving birth to Uthumphon, and everyone who had known her always commented on how much he resembled her—he had her eyes and smile. Perhaps that was why he was his father's favorite. Whatever the reason, Thammathibet had always been jealous, and the two of them weren't terribly close. Instead, Thammathibet had rebelled against their father, shirking his duties and sullying the family's reputation through his drunken antics.

But they were the royal family, rulers by decree of the spirits, who had given their ancestors the Jade Mask, or what was now known within the kingdom as the Mask of Succession. When his father passed, the abbot would place the mask on his brother, who would then succeed him as ruler.

And Uthumphon would be sworn to obey his elder brother, despite his unworthiness.

It gnawed at him, yet it was tradition.

And tradition was just that for a reason—it was never broken.

He sprinted up the palace steps and rushed through the doors opened by servants on either side. He raced up the wide stairs to the second floor then down the hall toward his father's chambers. One of the guards was about to open the door for him but he stopped the man with a wave of his hand. He halted, catching his breath for a moment, hunched over as he gripped his knees. A servant appeared holding a tray with flavored water. He drained the cup then straightened himself before nodding at the guard.

The door opened and Uthumphon stepped inside, the door immediately closing behind him. His father was on the large bed. Two servants were in the corners pulling on cords linked to the overhead fans, while two more busied themselves doing things he wasn't concerned about. There was only one servant he cared to hear from, and that was the family's personal physician, a native of Portugal, now leaning over his father.

"How is he?" asked Uthumphon, his voice low, respectful.

Dr. Ferreira glanced over his shoulder. "Recovering."

Uthumphon rounded the bed, opposite the side Ferreira occupied, and gasped at how pale and weak his father appeared. "What happened?"

"An attack of the heart, I suspect. He's been complaining of chest pains for months now. I've instructed him to be careful and to take it easy on the indulgences, but you know your father."

Uthumphon frowned and sat on the edge of the bed. "Yes, he ignores everyone's advice and does what he wants."

"It's what makes a great leader," said his father, the voice weak but still filled with the wisdom Uthumphon had known from birth.

"I thought you were asleep," said Ferreira.

"Sometimes it's wise to let others believe one can't hear them, so they reveal the secrets they might keep to themselves."

Ferreira grunted. "Well, you know me, and I know you, Your Majesty. You've always asked me to tell you the truth as I know it, and the truth is this. You have had an attack of the heart. It has weakened you considerably. As to whether you will live, I cannot say. The fact you are still alive is a good sign, and the next day will tell. If you are still with us tomorrow evening, I suspect you will be with us for a while longer. You will need to rest, remain calm, drink plenty of fluids—non-alcoholic—and eat plenty of fruit and vegetables. Avoid salt, as it causes you to retain water, and right now we want to flush your system of the evils within."

His father eyed the physician. "If we do all these things, will we live?"

Ferreira shrugged. "That is up to the spirits." He leaned in, wagging a finger. "Piss them off by ignoring my advice, and they just might make an example of you."

His father chuckled. "It's a good thing our wife liked you, otherwise we might have had you killed long ago for your familiarity."

Ferreira held up his hands, backing away slightly with a wry smile. "Killing me is your right, Your Majesty, and when the physician who replaces me is told I was killed because I didn't give the king the advice he wanted to hear, I am quite certain you will be told to ignore everything I said and to enjoy yourself, for you survived. And then you will be joining me in the afterlife the next day."

His father laughed, reaching out for Uthumphon's hand. He took it. "This is the key to ruling well. Find advisors you can trust, who will tell you the truth rather than what you want to hear. Only then can you rule wisely, for decisions can only be made with good information informing them." He turned to Ferreira. "What now?"

"I will take my leave of you, Your Majesty, and return in an hour to check on you. Get your rest, stay calm, eat and drink wisely, and I think your chances are very good."

The door burst open and Prince Thammathibet barged in. "Father! Are you all right?"

Ferreira glanced at Uthumphon then leaned closer to the king, lowering his voice. "Most of all, remain calm." He left the room, closing the door behind him, leaving Thammathibet to occupy his place.

"So, what's happened?"

Uthumphon responded. "Father has had an attack of the heart. He must remain *calm* and get as much rest as he can."

"Nonsense! He appears well to me."

"Then you are a blind fool. Dr. Ferreira says the next day is critical."
Uthumphon leaned closer. "If there is anything you require, Father, let
me know. We will take our leave of you now so you can rest. I'll leave
instructions with the servants as to what Dr. Ferreira said."

Their father closed his eyes and nodded. "Very well."

"But, Father! This is nonsense! A little food, a little drink, a good
massage. That's all you need."

"Leave me."

Uthumphon rose from his perch on the bed and headed for the
door, beckoning Thammathibet to follow. His brother frowned. "Fine,
but mark my words, in a few days we'll be laughing about this."

They exited the room and the guard closed the door. Uthumphon
flagged down his father's man. "He's not to be disturbed by anyone
except his physician unless he asks for someone personally. Bring him
plenty of drink, but nothing alcoholic, and food—nothing too salty. He
must get his rest and remain calm." He glanced at the pacing
Thammathibet. "No business of the kingdom, and that includes visits
by well-wishers. His physician will visit him regularly and keep us
posted. Understood?"

The man bowed deeply. "Completely, Your Highness." His eyes
flicked toward Thammathibet. "And family?"

Uthumphon picked up on the subtle implication. Thammathibet
caused nothing but stress for anyone he was around, and had likely
contributed to the current situation. "No family, not even me or my
brother. Agreed, Thammathibet?"

Thammathibet pursed his lips, staring at him before storming off. "Fine!" he shouted over his shoulder.

Uthumphon patted his father's man on the shoulder. "Good thinking," he whispered with a smile. "I'll be in my chambers. Do not hesitate to call on me should there be any problems."

Another bow. "Of course, Your Highness, thank you, Your Highness."

Uthumphon headed down the long hall toward the suite reserved for him that included bedchambers but also an office for him to conduct his business. He waved off his servants as he entered, and retreated to his bedchambers, staring out the window at the gardens below.

And his brother, who might be king in the coming hours, laughing with his friends and cavorting with a harlot not his wife.

May the spirits help us should he become our king.

Khwae Noi Tributary Dig Site
Kanchanaburi District, Thailand
Present Day, Three Days Earlier

Professor Chayan Bunthan gently reached down and used his fingers to push away the mud from the edge of the small piece of exposed jade. It revealed an even bigger portion below the surface, and his heart pounded a little harder as his team members, along with the visiting schoolchildren, leaned closer, everyone as excited as he was.

To this point, the dig site had been a fascinating glimpse into what life was like several centuries ago in this area. A recent river diversion for a hydroelectric project had dried up the river and revealed a village, buried for hundreds of years, all evidence suggesting it had been lost in a calamity as opposed to abandonment.

It was a window into how peasant farmers and fishermen lived at the time, and it reminded him in some ways of Pompeii. There, people had died from the gasses and were preserved by the gently falling ash.

Here, they died fleeing a wall of water. The village was heavily damaged, yet much remained, preserved in the now drying mud.

They were in the middle of nowhere, the area very poor, and the excitement of having a team from Bangkok here had drawn some attention, including from the local schools. They had already had several tours come through over the past week, and he loved taking the time to show the children around, teaching them a bit about their history, and of archaeology.

And it had been one of these students that had discovered the piece of jade sticking out of the ground on a practice grid set up for them. It was the first thing of potential monetary value they had found, and exactly the type of find they *didn't* want word of spreading, as it might attract the wrong element.

He had to play this carefully. A shard of jade was nothing. A curiosity with minimal value. A jade carving, especially something large, could be worth a fortune to someone living in abject poverty, and might spur rumors that there was more to be found. The locals could descend on the dig site and tear it apart if they thought their lives could be changed by finding something.

He shoved his finger deeper into the mud, tracing the fragment, and hid his excitement as his fingertip continued to sense the smooth stone. He couldn't proceed. It was too dangerous. He sat upright and threw his hands up in defeat as he rose. "Sorry, folks, just another piece of pottery. It was just painted green." A round of groans from the children had him forcing a smile to fit the lie. "Now, now, there's no reason to be disappointed. You children found an artifact we didn't

12

know was there until today. I'll tell you what. When we excavate it and clean it up, I'll let your teacher know, and you can come back to see what you found. Sound good?"

Cheers erupted and their teacher smiled gratefully at him as he was helped out of the hole by one of his university-aged students. "Thank you so much for sharing your time with us," said Miss Achara Panya, a beautiful woman with a bookish charm that Bunthan had to admit he was attracted to, even if she were ten years his junior. He had lost his wife in a car accident several years ago and hadn't dated since, instead throwing himself into his work. It had been a long time since he had been attracted to anyone, and for some inexplicable reason, he found Achara intoxicating.

"No need to thank me. It's been my pleasure. And I did mean what I said. When we clean it up, we'll have you all back."

"The children will be thrilled, I'm sure."

He took a chance, having noticed no wedding band. "And will you?"

She smiled, turning her head away slightly. "I will be as well, I'm sure."

He beamed at her as he walked her back to the beat-up bus the children had arrived in. "Please forgive me if I'm being too forward, but is there a Mr. Panya?"

"No." She gestured at his hand. "But there *is* a Mrs. Bunthan."

He reached for the ring, giving it a twist, having forgotten he was still wearing it. "There was. She died three years ago."

She paused, placing her hand on his arm. "I'm so sorry."

13

He shrugged, tapping the ring. "I guess you never really get over such a thing, and I never saw any reason to stop wearing the ring." He sighed. "Perhaps it's time."

She stared up at him with a smirk. "Perhaps it is, if you're going to hit on women."

His jaw dropped. "Oh my, am I that obvious?"

"You're definitely out of practice."

He chuckled. "I didn't mean to offend you."

She laughed. "You didn't offend me, Professor." She stopped as they reached the bus. "I understand you are staying here?"

"Yes. We're on a very small budget. If we used any of it toward accommodations, we'd have nothing left to feed ourselves."

"It must be very uncomfortable."

"You have no idea."

"Then might I suggest dinner? My parents own a small restaurant in town."

"That would be lovely. But meeting your parents on a first date?"

"Oh, they're traditionalists. There was going to be a chaperone regardless. This way they get to meet you and assess your intentions toward me."

He scratched the back of his neck, suddenly nervous. "I feel like I'm a teenage boy again."

She giggled and pulled out a piece of paper, writing something on it before handing it to him. "This is how to find it. Say, seven tonight?"

"I'll be there."

She climbed on the bus and it pulled away. He waved at her, the children returning it for her, but the smile she shot at him as he caught her last glimpse had his stomach in knots as both guilt and excitement gripped him.

"Sir?"

Bunthan turned to see one of his students, Sanun, standing behind him, grinning. "Umm, yes?"

"She's a hottie. I can't believe you asked her out."

Bunthan cleared his throat, glancing about. "Keep that to yourself."

"It's good for you, Professor. It's been three years. She would want you to move on, to be happy again."

He regarded Sanun, his prize pupil that had been with him for years, and there when he received the news of his wife's death. "Who says I'm not happy?"

"Everyone."

Bunthan pursed his lips. "Everyone?"

"Yes, Professor. No one wants to say anything, but you work too hard, you never have fun." Sanun gestured toward the now departed bus. "She could be good for you. Have some fun tonight, remember what it's like to spend time with a pretty girl." He wagged a finger. "And don't feel guilty about being happy. It's all right to move on."

Bunthan stared at the much younger man, then realized he wasn't so young anymore. "When did you get so old and wise?"

Sanun shrugged. "Good mentor, I suppose."

Bunthan chuckled. "Perhaps." He headed back toward the jade discovery. "Please keep this to yourself. I don't want the entire camp discussing my love life."

Sanun lowered his voice. "I think it might be a little too late for that. Everyone saw how you two were looking at each other."

Bunthan noticed several staring with smiles. "Lovely. I'm now the camp gossip." He pointed at the hole as the others gathered around. "As I'm sure you've all suspected, I told a little fib to our visitors."

"What did she say?" asked Suchin, one of his female grad students.

He eyed her. "She thanked me for allowing them to visit."

"By writing it down?"

His cheeks flushed as he realized he still had the piece of paper Achara had given him, gripped in his hand. He stuffed it in his pocket. "Fine. You'll all know before the sun goes down, because Sanun here can't keep a secret. She invited me to have dinner with her"—hoots and other inappropriate sounds and comments erupted from his far too young companions—"at her *parents'* restaurant. Very innocent, very proper, I can assure you."

"Good for you, Professor," said Suchin. "She's cute!"

He held up both hands, palms out. "All right, all right, that's enough." He pointed at the hole and the shard of jade still protruding from it. "Back to business. *That* is obviously not part of a clay pot. It's clearly jade. It could have monetary value, so I didn't want any locals seeing it, because word could spread." He hopped down then kneeled beside the exposed edge. "Now, let's see what we actually have here."

And after a few minutes of careful digging with his hands, he had revealed enough to know what it was.

And that they were all in terrible danger should word get out.

Royal Palace

Ayutthaya, Ayutthaya Kingdom

April 26, 1758

Prince Uthumphon entered his father's bedchambers and suppressed a gasp at the sight that lay before him. His father appeared near death, his cheeks sallow, his skin ashen, any life that had been there just yesterday now gone. It was heartbreaking. There was little doubt now that his father wouldn't be long with them, and might not even make the night. And he assumed that's why he had been summoned, against the physician's orders.

He forced a smile as he approached his father's bedside. "How are you feeling?"

His father's head turned toward him and a weak smile greeted him. "How do I look?"

Uthumphon's eyes burned and tears threatened to escape, for he couldn't bear to tell his father the truth. Oh, how he wished at this moment to have the capacity to lie with ease as his brother did, yet he

18

couldn't. It wasn't in his nature. He had always told the truth, sometimes to his own detriment. He never got away with anything as a child, for guilt would rack him to such a degree that a stern look would have the floodgates opening.

So today, he said nothing.

"That bad?"

The tears rolled and he plunked down on the bed, his shoulders rounded as his back faced his father. Men weren't supposed to cry. Certainly not heirs to the throne. If his brother were to die, and he was forced to become king, what would his subjects think of a leader, chosen by the spirits, who cried?

A hand touched his back for a brief moment and he turned to see his father's arm flop onto the bed, the effort having taxed the poor man far more than it should have. Uthumphon wiped the tears from his cheeks and sniffed heavily.

"I'm sorry, Father. I know I shouldn't behave like this, but…"

"It's all right, my son. I too cried at your grandfather's bedside when he died."

Uthumphon's eyes shot wide. "You? You cried?"

His father smiled slightly. "Yes. All men cry at some point in their lives. Some resist it, where tears never flow, but they are crying nonetheless. Others cry at the sunset of a difficult day. There is no shame in it, though as the future king, you must keep such emotions hidden from your subjects. While the women may worship you for having a heart, the men, who share such emotions yet hide them, will lose respect."

Uthumphon grunted. "Well, there's no risk of that happening. Thammathibet will rule, I am certain, for a long time, then his son will become king. I will be happy to remain in the background, playing my small part."

His father gripped his hand, the squeeze of the fingers barely felt. "No, my son. I have made my decision. *You* will inherit my throne, not your brother."

A wave of nausea swept through him as sweat broke out on his forehead and upper lip, beads trickling down his spine. "Wh-what?"

"You will be king after I'm gone."

Uthumphon's jaw slackened as palpitations ravaged his chest. The pounding in his ears was almost overwhelming, and he felt faint. Both arms darted out, gripping the bed on either side as he struggled to steady himself. This couldn't be. The eldest son always succeeded the death of the father. As far as he was aware, this cycle had never been broken, not in all of the years of the kingdom.

And there was only one explanation for what had just been said, and that realization had his nerves steadying and his heart settling. He wiped his brow with the back of his hand and smiled at his father, though there was no hiding the sadness that gripped him, knowing the man's mind was going.

"You're mistaken, Father. You know that Thammathibet is the eldest and must inherit. I cannot take your place unless Thammathibet dies without a male heir."

"That is where *you* are mistaken."

Uthumphon's eyebrows narrowed, his chest tightening once again. "What do you mean?"

"It is *tradition* that the eldest inherits the throne, not law. All is dictated by the Mask of Succession. He who possesses it after the king has died, becomes king himself. All that matters is that he is part of the royal bloodline and male. Hierarchy is of no importance."

Uthumphon's eyebrows shot up. "Surely this can't be true."

"It is, and always has been. Sadly, this is the first time in the history of our bloodline where the eldest son must not inherit the throne. Should your brother succeed me, I fear it would mean the end of all that our family has built over the generations, and there will be nothing left for his own son to inherit." His father gripped his hand, some of the strength he was accustomed to, returned. "Son, it is imperative that your brother never sit on the throne. It will be the end of all we have built."

Acton/Palmer Residence

St. Paul, Maryland

Present Day

Archaeology Professor James Acton plopped onto the couch, exhausted. They had closed escrow on their new house a few weeks ago, and had finally finished moving in. Yet were they really finished? He doubted it. His wife, Archaeology Professor Laura Palmer, dropped beside him, curling her legs and snuggling up next to him. He placed his arm over her shoulders and squeezed her tight as he stared at their new surroundings.

"I can't believe we finally did it," he sighed.

"Neither can I. Do you think it's too big?"

Acton grunted. "Of course it's too big. You could fit my old house and your London flat in here, and still have room for a basketball court. But there wasn't much choice. Everything on the market was either just a variation of what we already had, or a monster."

She stroked his chest absentmindedly. "It's a lot of house, but we can afford it, and it will be fun to fill it. I've already picked out my office. You?"

"Yup. I wonder if we picked the same one. Front of the house?"

"Yes."

"Left corner."

She sat up, staring at him. "Yes."

"Second—"

"Floor! Yes!" Her lower lip thrust out. "Not fair! I picked it the moment I saw it."

"So did I."

"When?"

"When I said 'dibs.'"

"Dibs?"

"Hey, if you're going to live in America, you need to learn our customs."

"You're mean."

He grinned. "Yet you still want me." He turned on the smolder. "Don't ya, baby?"

She giggled. "You're incorrigible."

"Hey, no big words." He rose and extended a hand. "How about we go buff the floors in your new office?"

"*My* new office?"

"Yeah, I was only joking. I knew you wanted it from the moment we stepped in the room."

She took his hand and rose, grabbing him and dropping a kiss for the ages on him. She stared into his eyes. "What was that about buffing the floors?"

A toothy grin. "I'm thinking every room in the house should be broken in." He leaned closer. "How about we start with Hugh's room? It will be our dirty little secret."

She playfully slapped his chest. "You *are* incorrigible." Her face brightened and she hopped on her toes. "Let's!"

He grinned to himself at what was about to happen, then groaned when her phone vibrated on the table. She grabbed it and read the message, and her excitement grew—so he knew it had nothing to do with sex with him. "What is it?"

"Oh, this is wonderful. I've been working on this for over a year."

He eyed her. "You've been keeping secrets from me?"

She dismissed his joke as if it were serious with a wave of her hand. "No, no, nothing like that. I just didn't want to get anyone's hopes up."

Now she had him curious. "What is it?"

"You know how Mai has been feeling homesick and misses her father?"

"Of course." His jaw dropped. "Don't tell me you figured out a way to get him here."

She shook her head. "I wish! No, nothing so grandiose, I'm afraid. Mary has confirmed he is blacklisted and will never be granted permission to leave the country, but he does have free movement again as of a couple of weeks ago. She had one of her contacts in Hanoi visit him, and all the arrangements have been made."

He still had no clue what was going on. "What arrangements?"

She wagged her phone as she hopped up and down. "The visas just came through for all of us."

He held out a hand, calming her down. "Listen, you're leaving out an awful lot of information here. Visas for what?"

"We're all going to Cambodia. Mai's going to be able to see her father again!"

Royal Palace

Ayutthaya, Ayutthaya Kingdom

April 26, 1758

Abbot Luang entered the bedchambers of his king, his curiosity at having been summoned answered when he laid eyes upon the man. The king was dying, of that, there could be no doubt. He had seen those at death's door far too many times in his life, and had been there when this man's father had died.

And it was a joyous occasion for the individual, though a tragedy for those they left behind. It meant a journey into the afterlife, and while time on this earth was a gift from the spirits, Nirvana was their karmic reward for a life well lived, and this man who had ruled them for decades had indeed lived a good life. The kingdom had thrived under his guidance, the people were happy, and their enemies dared not challenge them.

Life here was good.

And it was thanks to this man.

And when he died, which appeared to be not far off, it would indeed be a tragedy for his subjects, especially with what Luang knew of the eldest son.

Thammathibet was a selfish imp, who cared not for his people, nor appeared to have the mental capacity to rule. He was obsessed with the pleasures available to him due to his position. He ate and drank to excess, bedded a different woman every night, and shirked the duties expected of the king's eldest son.

It would indeed be a tragedy when he inherited.

But it was the will of the spirits, and surely the spirits couldn't be wrong. As a man of religion, he had to believe that if the spirits wanted Thammathibet to become king, and rule with ineptitude, then it must not be because the spirits were in error in choosing him, but instead, because they were punishing the people.

The population was happy. Very happy. That came with prosperity, and those in the kingdom led far better lives than their neighbors who toiled under lesser monarchs. And perhaps they shared in some of the decadence that their future king enjoyed. Perhaps, when bellies were always full, it left time for idle hands to turn to evil. He had seen the drunks in the streets himself, the women trading their bodies for money rather than finding a husband to take care of them.

There was much sin in the kingdom, and perhaps Thammathibet as king was the way to cure them of it. Under his inept leadership, surely the realm would falter, the prosperity enjoyed today would become a thing of the past, and the spare money for alcohol and women would dry up. Perhaps it would lead to a purification of his beloved people through suffering.

"Come closer, Abbot."

Luang edged toward the bed, his head bowed, his hands clasped in front of him. "You summoned me, Your Majesty?"

"We have an important matter to discuss."

"Yes?"

"We are dying. we doubt we will see tonight's sunset, let alone tomorrow's sunrise."

Luang frowned, edging even closer as his fears were confirmed. The kingdom was about to suffer, perhaps for decades. "Surely the physicians can do something?"

The king shook his head, the motion barely noticeable. "They've done all they can. It is in the hands of the spirits now, and we hear them beckoning. But before we die, there is work to be done, and we require your assistance."

"Anything, Your Majesty."

"It is about who will inherit our throne."

Luang's eyes narrowed. "Your Majesty?"

"Thammathibet cannot sit on the throne after we are gone. It will mean the destruction of the kingdom. Our enemies will sweep in and conquer us, and our people will suffer should he be their leader."

A pit formed in Luang's stomach at the words. For a king to say such things about his son was unheard of. Most fathers he passed on the street wouldn't say such things. The king was chosen by the spirits, and Thammathibet was the eldest son, therefore he had been chosen. If the spirits didn't want him, for better or for worse, he never would have been born.

He swallowed. "I don't understand, Your Majesty."

"Thammathibet cannot inherit. We have decided that Uthumphon will be king after we are gone."

Luang gasped then slapped a hand over his mouth. "Forgive me, Your Majesty, but I…I'm not sure what to say." He drew a deep breath. "You want your youngest, Uthumphon, to be your heir, not your eldest, Thammathibet?"

"Exactly."

"But, Your Majesty, it can't be. The eldest always inherits. It has always been this way."

"Yes, it has, but never before have we faced a situation where the eldest son is so unworthy of becoming king."

"But tradition—"

"Means nothing. *Law* is everything. We both know that it is he who possesses the Mask of Succession that inherits the throne, as long as that person is of the royal bloodline if possible, and a male. It doesn't matter what order of birth, nor does it even matter if they are the son of the late king, as long as they are in possession of the mask."

Luang gulped as his mind raced. He had read the scrolls that covered the history of the kingdom, and those that had preceded its current incarnation. The mask had always been handed down to the eldest son, though there had been several occasions where there were no male children, so a nephew would be named king. In all cases, it was the senior abbot that would place the mask on the dead king's face,

29

recite the funeral rites, then place the mask on the heir. From that moment on, as long as that person was alive, they were king, even if the mask was taken by someone else.

As long as they were alive.

"How? I mean, do you intend to kill…" He stood there, flustered for a moment. "Thammathibet will never agree to this," he finally sputtered.

"What Thammathibet wants is of no concern to us. All that matters is that the mask is placed on Uthumphon's face at the end of the ceremony, and not Thammathibet's. Can we count on you?"

Luang closed his eyes for a moment, steadying his pounding heart before nodding. "I live to serve."

"Very good. Then bring the mask here immediately. We suspect the hours grow short for us, and we don't want any delays."

Luang bowed. "I shall return with great haste, Your Majesty." He backed out of the room and didn't turn until the doors closed. He hurried from the palace, sweat soaking his body as his pulse hammered and his mind struggled to make sense of what was happening.

His king had ordered him to break with centuries of tradition.

And he wasn't certain it was his place to allow it to happen.

Muban Chong Sadao

Kanchanaburi District, Thailand

Present Day

Bunthan parked the van provided by the university for the dig and sat behind the wheel for a moment, ignoring the small restaurant with patio in front of him. This was a poor town, very poor, the poverty he witnessed every time he came here heartbreaking. But that was the way things were in rural Thailand. Yet none of that was on his mind right now. It should be Achara, but it wasn't.

It was what they had found.

It could be only one thing. It matched the historical descriptions, yet it had been lost long before photography, so there was no way to be sure. Yet how many could there be? It was a jade mask that covered the entire face, intricately carved by what was clearly a skilled artisan, trimmed with gold, and encrusted with priceless jewels that covered its full surface.

31

There was little doubt they had found what had been lost for centuries, what had led to the downfall of an entire kingdom, and changed the history of his country forever.

They had found the Mask of Succession.

It was a stunning find, certainly the biggest of his career, and while it should excite him, it instead terrified him. It was priceless from a historical standpoint, but the jewels alone were worth millions. The mask itself, intact, could sell for an unfathomable amount on the black market, yet that would require a sophisticated thief.

Here, he feared the local gangs.

He had to get the mask to safety, back to Bangkok, before word leaked. He trusted his students and staff, but in today's social media-obsessed culture, he feared one of them might snap a photo and upload it. Their budget was small, but he had arranged for a Starlink terminal to provide them with good Internet access rather than risk a mutiny.

And it meant an upload could happen at any moment.

You should have shut it down before you left.

He grunted.

Then you'd definitely have a mutiny on your hands.

Achara appeared in the doorway to the restaurant and smiled at him, beckoning him to come inside. He sighed, his stomach churning as his mind returned to the other thing making this an incredibly difficult day.

The restart of his love-life.

You can do this.

He stared down at his wedding band then twisted it off, placing it in the cupholder. He didn't want it anywhere near him, not tonight. He climbed out and shut the door, smiling at her. She was gorgeous. Unbelievably gorgeous, yet in a simple way. In the city, she would be considered plain. Not enough makeup, hair too flat, clothing too basic, and nothing but a simple handcrafted necklace for accessories.

She was perfect.

Just like his wife when they first met.

Bile filled his mouth as guilt swept over him, but he swallowed and forced a smile. "You look lovely tonight."

She clutched her hands together in front of her. "And you look handsome."

He stared down at himself and chuckled. "You're looking at a man who bathed in what's left of the river, and was dressed by his female students after they saw what I was going to wear."

"Well, they did an excellent job."

He shrugged. "Then forget what I said. I take all the credit."

She giggled and beckoned him inside. "Come. My parents are eager to meet you."

The next two hours were a whirlwind, and he forgot his troubles concerning the mask, instead enjoying an incredible evening with the lovely Achara and her parents, who kept a close eye on them while serving their customers, often joining them during lulls.

And they were wonderful as well. Simple folk with plenty of questions, mostly about his background, why he wasn't already married, how long it had been since his wife died, what kind of a provider he

33

would make. Standard stuff of parents everywhere, he supposed, though the questions did add pressure to the evening. He had the distinct impression that if they approved of him, they'd be entering marriage negotiations.

"Forgive them," said Achara as her mother left the table to greet new customers. "I realize what this is, even if they do not."

He regarded her. "And what is this?"

"A lonely man looking to spend some time with a woman, to take his mind off his problems."

He took her hand, a loud clearing of the throat from the front of the house nixing the action. "This is not a one-night-stand as the Americans might call it. I like you, that's why I talked to you earlier. And after this evening, I realize I was right."

She stared at her glass, gripped in front of her. "What are you saying?"

"I'm saying I'd like to see you again."

She peered up at him, keeping her chin low. "Really?"

"Of course. Only if you want to see me, though."

"I would love—like—to see you again. But…"

His chest tightened. "But what?"

"Where is this going?"

"I'm going to be here for months. Why don't we see how things go before we start talking about our future together?"

Her chin pressed even further into her chest. "Things are simpler here. It's not like in the city."

34

"I understand. And that's part of why I like you. It was the same with my wife. She was from a small village much like this. It was one of the things I loved about her. She didn't care about the city. She just wanted a simple life."

Achara's head rose. "But you would expect me to move to the city, wouldn't you?"

He smiled. "I suppose I would, if we were to be married, but let's not worry about that tonight. Let's get to know each other. You might find in time that you don't like me."

Her head again dropped. "I can't imagine that."

A motorcycle engine cut through the dusk, followed by several more. Everyone tensed, including Achara.

"What's wrong?"

"Hopefully it's nothing. They normally don't come in here."

"Who?"

"Red Wa wannabees. They're a gang in this area that like to think they're part of Red Wa. You know, the organized crime gang? They ride around on their motorcycles, harassing people, drinking, stealing. They're very bad, but normally they stay out of here. You saw my father. He's a big man."

Achara's father emerged from the kitchen in the back as the motorcycles came to a halt outside. He had a meat cleaver in one hand, and a carving fork in the other. He was a terrifying sight, and Bunthan gulped at the prospect of having a man such as this as his father-in-law. The door swung open and a man entered, all swagger and no substance. He pointed at Achara's mother.

"Get me a beer, woman."

"Get the hell out of here!" shouted Mr. Panya. "You know you and your kind aren't welcome here."

The man pointed at Achara and she whimpered. "I have business with your daughter."

Bunthan tensed and was about to stand up to place himself between Achara and the new arrival when she hissed, "Don't." He stopped himself, and the man sauntered over with his pelvis shoved forward as if the cock-of-the-walk.

"I'm here to talk about my daughter with her teacher."

Achara trembled, and from the reaction of the entire restaurant, it was with reason. An arrogant bastard like this wouldn't bother him in the city. He had had enough students over the years much like this parasite. But here, in the jungle, life was valued differently. In the city, most men like this that he encountered had something to live for, had goals in life that could come to a crashing halt if they followed through on their threats.

Here, this man could kill everyone in the restaurant and just leave, without worrying about the authorities ever finding him, and if they did, he could either pay them off, or die in a blaze of glory, ending a life not worth living.

He had to keep the situation from escalating.

He extended a hand. "Hi there, I'm Professor Bunthan from Silpakorn University. I had a group of students at my dig site today. Was your daughter among them?"

The man regarded him with disdain, ignoring the hand. "Yes." He grabbed a chair from a nearby table and sat, his legs straddling the back. "So, you're the one who lied to my daughter." He grabbed Bunthan's beer and took a swig. "You shouldn't lie to children."

Bunthan suppressed the urge to gulp. "I lied?"

Another swig. A big one. A phone was pulled out and a picture brought up. "My daughter took this photo. That's jade! It's no clay pot like you said."

Sweat trickled down Bunthan's back as his greatest fear manifested before him. There was no way he could admit the truth. He instead played along. He held out his hand. "May I?"

The phone was slapped in his palm and he zoomed in, his mind racing for a plausible explanation for what was clearly jade. He smiled. "Oh, *that* pot. No, it is just a clay pot." He pointed at the distinctive green poking out from the mud. "This was fired in a kiln. They formed the pot then fired it to make it hard, then they would dip it in a heated glaze that once cooled, hardens into a glass and appears shiny like this." He handed the phone back. "I can assure you, sir, that this is just a clay pot with a green glaze to make it smooth. Nothing more."

The man stared at him for a moment, the restaurant collectively holding its breath, before he finally rose, shoving his phone in his pocket. "Kids! What do they know?" He stabbed a finger at both of them. "But my little girl found that, so if it's worth anything, I want it."

"It is worthless, I assure you. Only someone like me would find any value in it."

37

The man finished the beer then slammed the empty bottle onto the table. He wagged a finger. "You better not be lying."

"I'm not, I assure you."

The man grunted and stumbled from the restaurant, no one relaxing a muscle until the motorcycles faded in the distance.

Achara sighed, reaching out and gripping his hand. "That was so brave!"

He squeezed her hand as he exhaled, his entire body trembling for a moment. His potential in-laws rushed over and he withdrew his hand, the bloody meat cleaver looming large in his field of vision. "Are you all right, Professor?" asked Mr. Panya.

"Yes, I'm fine. A little on edge, obviously, but I'll be fine."

"Get him another beer." Mr. Panya then launched into a tirade about their visitor, a man named Zhao, who had been harassing the town for years. Most of what was said was lost in the fog of the situation as the adrenaline pumping through his veins waned. His mind could only focus on one thing.

He had fooled a drunk man tonight, but tomorrow, in the light of day, would Zhao take another look at the photo so clearly of a piece of jade?

And would he pay the dig site a visit with his gang?

He had to get the mask to safety, yet he wasn't sure how, for if he left, they would surely know something was wrong and pursue him.

What am I supposed to do?

Royal Gardens

Ayutthaya, Ayutthaya Kingdom

April 26, 1758

Prince Thammathibet groaned in pleasure as his favorite masseuse, Suriya, kneaded his shoulders. He took a swig of his drink, the bite harsh, like his mood. He should be happy. He was young, good-looking, rich, powerful—everything any young man could want. He led a good life thanks to his position, and made certain he enjoyed every moment.

But it was all about to come to an end.

His father was dying. In fact, he might already be dead and the news simply hadn't reached him yet. He hated his father. Anything he did was never good enough for the man, though in his father's defense, he never put much effort into anything except partying. He was young. This was his time to enjoy life, and when the time came, when he was well into his thirties or forties, he would happily take over when his father passed.

But not now, not at 25. His father should have at least a couple more decades of life in him, but if Ferreira were to be believed, and the family physician was rarely wrong, he wouldn't see tomorrow.

He stared at the pool, filled with friends and local girls brought in for the daily parties, and sighed. It was over.

"Something wrong?" asked Suriya as she continued to work her magic.

"My father is dying."

Her fingers froze as she gasped. "The king is dying?"

He reached back and slapped one of her hands and she resumed. "Yes. He'll probably be dead before the day is out."

"That's horrible! I'm so sorry to hear that."

"I bet you are."

Her fingers slowed. "What do you mean by that?"

He bolted to his feet. "I mean, you like him, don't you? You can't imagine him not being your king! You're scared that when I become king, I'll ruin everything!"

She stared at him wide-eyed, her mouth agape. "I said no such thing! I think you'll make a fine king. I just meant it must be sad to lose your father. I'm just not used to referring to him as anything but the king."

He glared at her, then spun, shooting daggers at his so-called friends as they judged him with their icy stares. "You all think it, don't you? You all think I'm not worthy of being king. You're all worried what will happen when I take my father's place."

Nobody said anything, most diverting their gaze, the cowards unwilling to challenge him, for they all knew that tomorrow he could have them killed with a snap of his fingers. He drew a deep breath, exhaling loudly as he thought about what was truly happening. Tomorrow, perhaps even tonight, he would be king. It meant he was all-powerful. He was the law, and no one could deny him any want or desire. Once king, he could still party like he always had. What his subjects thought be damned.

He would have ultimate power.

The thought had his anger turning to excitement, and for the first time since the news about his father, he wasn't scared, he wasn't leery—he wanted it. He wanted the power, the adoration. He might have to quench his public appetites somewhat, but it didn't mean he couldn't enjoy the delights of the female populace in the privacy of his own bedchambers.

He dropped back into his chair and Suriya resumed the massage. He waved a hand at the crowd, deciding he better start acting like a king. "I'm sorry, everyone. I guess my father's imminent death has me more upset than I realized."

"I'm sorry if I said anything to upset you," said Suriya.

He turned back to face her and smiled. "You said nothing improper." He again waved his hand at the others. "Please, continue. We're here to enjoy ourselves. And while we will soon have something to mourn, we will also have something to celebrate. We will all weep at my father the king's passing, then we will rejoice in my coronation."

His best friend, Aphon, thrust his drink in the air. "To the future king!"

Cheers erupted and Thammathibet smiled, a shiver rushing through him as his name was shouted with a reverence he had never before heard. If this was what it felt like to be king, then perhaps what was soon to come wouldn't be so bad after all.

He spotted the senior abbot, Luang, beckoning him near the gate that surrounded the pool area. He couldn't recall ever seeing the man here, and with what was going on, it must be related to his father. He rose and strode swiftly toward the man. "What is it, Abbot?"

Luang glanced about nervously. "I must speak with you. In private."

"Of course." Thammathibet led the elderly man away from the gathering and into the pool house, making certain it was empty. "What is it you need to speak to me about? Is it about the king?"

Luang's chin was pressed against his chest, his shoulders rolled forward as if he were about to say the most forbidden of things. "Yes."

"What is it?"

"I just spoke with the king, and..." The man's voice was quaking. He was terrified, something Thammathibet had never seen in the man.

"What has you so upset?"

"I shouldn't be telling you this. It is not my place, however, tradition dictates..."

Thammathibet was tiring of this. "Tradition dictates what?" he snapped.

Luang flinched and backed away a step.

42

Thammathibet repeated his question, this time with a forced calm. "Tradition dictates what?"

"That the eldest inherits the throne."

"Yes, we all know—" He stopped, his heart hammering as his eyebrows shot up. "Wait, are you suggesting—"

"The king has instructed me to give the Mask of Succession to your younger brother, not to you."

It was Thammathibet's turn to take an involuntary step back. "Wh-what?"

"He intends for Uthumphon to succeed him as king, not you."

Thammathibet dropped onto a nearby bench, his head shaking. "Can he do that? I thought tradition—"

"Tradition is not law. By tradition, the eldest son inherits, however, there have been cases through our history where there was no direct male heir, and someone else was chosen, usually a close male relative. The real tradition is that he who first wears the Mask of Succession after the king dies, becomes king until he himself dies."

Thammathibet stared at his feet, his head still shaking. "So, he can do this?"

"He is the king. He can do anything he wants."

"But once he's dead, you no longer have to obey his wishes."

Luang gasped at the very notion. "I must follow the wishes given to me by my king, until such time as there is a new king to countermand them. I *will* be giving the mask to your younger brother. I am bound by my oath."

Thammathibet sat back and regarded Luang with a deep frown. "Then why are you telling me this?"

"Tradition dictates you should be king. I believe in that tradition, despite…" His voice trailed off, and he turned slightly away.

"Despite the worthiness of he who should inherit?"

"I dare not say such a thing."

Thammathibet grunted. "You're not the only one who feels that way." He sighed. "Even I feel it."

Luang risked a glance. "Your Highness?"

Thammathibet exhaled loudly. "You and I both know that I am not ready to be king. I would make a terrible king. I had always assumed I would have time to grow into the role. Now that chance has been taken from me with my father's untimely demise."

"He's not dead yet."

"No, I suppose he's not, however, you wouldn't be here if you had any hope of him surviving much longer."

Luang said nothing, though responded with a single nod.

"Then why tell me? To what end?"

"Perhaps there is still time to change his mind." Luang finally met his gaze. "Should you wish to be king."

Acton/Palmer Residence

St. Paul, Maryland

Present Day

Interpol Agent Hugh Reading stared at his surroundings, shaking his head in disbelief. The size of the house his best friends now owned was immense by British standards, especially London standards, and he was happy for them. Laura had inherited an unfathomable amount of money when her tech-entrepreneur brother had died, yet had never taken up the opulent lifestyle it could have provided her.

It was one of the reasons he respected the two of them so much.

They were rich, but normal. Well, mostly normal. Normal people didn't keep running toward the danger, rather than away from it. He was thankful they had invited him to see the new house, and that they were staying put in nice, safe, simple Maryland, where there was little chance of getting into trouble.

"What do you think?" asked Acton. "A little bigger than we wanted, but once we're settled, it will start to feel like home."

Reading grunted. "Who's going to clean it?"

"We're getting a maid," echoed his friends, and he had to laugh.

"I think you might need *staff* with this place, not just a maid."

Acton scratched his chin. "I hadn't thought about that. That's so Downton Abbey."

Laura shrugged. "We'll figure it out." She held out a hand toward a set of stairs. "Let's get you settled in your room."

He followed them up the stairs, both of them carrying his luggage, much to his outward annoyance, though thankful for it. The years were creeping up on him, and everything ached these days. He sometimes wondered if life were worth living with the pain, but friends like this, and his son, kept him going.

But the job?

It was a desk job for the most part, but he didn't find it rewarding. The only sense of accomplishment he now had in life usually surrounded getting these two out of messes.

They walked down a ridiculously long hallway then Laura opened a door at the far end, pushing it aside. "Welcome to your new home away from home."

Acton beamed a smile at him, and Laura was as giddy as he had ever seen her.

And he was puzzled, his eyes narrowing.

He stepped inside and gasped. To call this a bedroom would be an insult to bedrooms the world over. It was a suite. Greeting him was a living area with a couch and chairs along with a large television. To his right was an open concept kitchenette, and through another door he could see a full bedroom with a king-sized bed.

"What's all this?" he asked as he spotted a photo of his son, Spencer, sitting on the fireplace mantle.

Acton squeezed his shoulder. "This is your home away from home. It's yours whenever you want to visit."

Laura wiped a tear. "No one will ever stay here except you, so if you want to change anything, just let us know. If you want to leave any personal items, feel free."

Reading's chest tightened and he squeezed his eyes shut. This couple had done so much for him over the years, but this was beyond anything he could have imagined. He sniffed. "Bollocks. You've made an old man cry."

Laura embraced him and he held her tight, grabbing Acton by the shoulder and giving him a shake. "We love you, Hugh. You know that."

He sighed, wiping his eyes dry with a knuckle. "You two are too good to me. I don't deserve this."

Laura gently pushed away, staring into his eyes. "You absolutely deserve this. You're family, and family should be together whenever possible. You can visit whenever you want, for as long as you want."

Acton wiped his own eyes dry. "And we've discussed it and agreed that if you want to retire here, or split your time between the UK and here, we'd love to have you."

Reading's shoulders shook and he turned away, ashamed of his emotional display. He was old school. Men didn't cry, men bottled up their emotions. But this was too much. Back home he was so alone. His son was busy with his life, he was divorced, he didn't socialize with anyone at work besides his partner, and she had her own life. His best friend from Scotland Yard was dead, and his mates had moved on with their lives.

It was painfully lonely at times.

He had grown very close to Acton and Laura over the years, and was even on friendly terms with some of the Delta Force team and CIA operatives that peppered their lives from time to time. Tommy and Mai were like grandchildren to him, and much to his astonishment, the idea of retiring in America rather than back home had appeal.

"You'd grow sick of me."

Acton laughed, slapping him on the back. "Not before you're sick of us." He stepped deeper into the suite. "You have everything here you'll need. You could hole up in here and never come out if you want. We intentionally picked this house because of this suite. We wanted you to feel like you had a home here, rather than being a guest."

He sighed heavily, his shoulders slumping. The generosity of his friends knew no bounds. They always invited him on their vacations, paying for everything, yet this was something more. They were always doing things for their students and strangers, never asking for any credit, never expecting any repayment.

They were generous beyond compare.

He stepped over to the kitchen and opened the fridge, frowning at the essentials filling the shelves. "What, no pints?"

Acton stepped over and opened a door under the counter he had mistaken for a dishwasher. "Beer fridge."

Reading laughed. "You've thought of everything."

"Wait until you see the shower. It's got—"

The wail of a siren interrupted them and they all stepped over to the window to see a firetruck rush past as a car pulled into their driveway.

"Oh, Mai and Tommy are here," said Laura as she bounced on her toes. "I can't wait to tell them the news!" She rushed from the room, leaving Acton to explain.

"She's got a surprise for Mai. Why don't we head downstairs, since this involves you, if you want?"

Reading tossed his head back and groaned. "What are you getting me into this time?"

Acton laughed and slapped him on the back as they headed for the stairs. "You'll see. Nothing crazy, nothing dangerous. Just a little bit of fun."

"Uh-huh. Why do I get the feeling I'm being set up?"

Acton flashed an innocent look. "I would never do anything like that."

"Bollocks." Reading smiled broadly at Tommy and Mai, giving the young man a hearty handshake and returning Mai's excited hug.

"Did you see your new room?" she asked, her eyes wide.

He nodded. "I did, but I don't think I'd call that a room. It's more like a flat."

Tommy agreed. "It's amazing! So, do you think you'll live there when you retire?"

Reading gave him a look. "Let's not be putting me out to pasture just yet, lad." He gestured toward the main entrance. "What was the firetruck for?"

"Your neighbor's car is on fire."

Laura gasped, her hand darting to her chest. "Oh no! I hope no one is hurt."

"It was in the driveway with a bunch of people standing around it. They didn't look panicked."

"Which house?" asked Acton.

"Two doors down, across the street. Big one with a gate."

Acton chuckled, elbowing Reading. "You know what they drive?"

Reading grunted. "In a neighborhood like this, I'm suspecting something more expensive than that beat-up beast you've got parked outside."

"Oh, it's a domestic sportscar, at least for you."

Reading laughed. "Spontaneous combustion. That's a new one, even for them."

Laura invited everyone into the living room with an extended arm. "Shall we?"

They stepped into the unfamiliar surroundings, and everyone stood about for a moment, wondering where they should sit. Their old home essentially had assigned seating since it was so familiar, but now everything was new. Acton went first, sitting on a couch, then Laura sat beside him. Tommy and Mai took a loveseat, and Reading chose what appeared to be a ridiculously comfortable chair.

He moaned.

"All right, *this* is where I'm retiring."

Acton laughed. "I thought you might like that, but I wanted to be sure. We'll show you the upholstery samples later so we can order one for your room."

Reading shook his head. "You've done too much already."

"It's already done. We just need you to pick the upholstery."

Mai giggled. "You should know by now that there's no fighting them."

Reading sighed, leaning his head back. "You're right. I don't know why I bother." He regarded Laura. "Now, enough about what you've done for me. I understand you have news?"

Laura smiled and leaned closer to Mai. "I have a surprise for you."

Tommy's face lit up. "Is it a chair like that?"

Laura swatted a hand at him. "Behave. Mai..." She choked up and Mai's eyes flooded.

"What is it?"

"We're all heading to Cambodia tomorrow."

Mai jerked back slightly. "Cambodia? Why?"

"We've—"

Acton interrupted. "*She*. This is all Laura's doing."

Laura smiled at him. "Very well. *I* have arranged for you to see your father."

Mai leaped to her feet, her eyes wide, her mouth agape. "What? Are you serious?"

"Yes. It's all been arranged. If everything goes to plan, you'll see him the day after tomorrow."

Mai hopped up and down with excitement, the poor girl having not seen her father in years, and resigned to the fact she likely would never see him again due to her political status. She leaned forward to hug Laura but stumbled, falling into her lap. They both laughed as they held each other, Tommy now on his feet as he extended a hand over them to thank Acton.

Reading smiled at the scene. Today was a good day. A very good day. He had been depressed lately, but his friends had certainly cured him of that, at least for now.

His smile turned into a frown.

"Wait a minute, did you say you got visas for *all* of us?"

Acton grinned. "Yes. You're coming with us, if you want."

Reading groaned. "Another hot, uncomfortable country. You nearly killed me with India."

"*We* didn't nearly kill you, the Chinese did."

"You were making a hell of an effort before they got involved."

Mai and Tommy returned to their seats and Laura attempted to make him feel a little better. "We'll leave here tomorrow, take the jet, and arrive in Phnom Penh the next morning."

He could already feel his ass and back protesting. "How many hours?"

"Almost a full day. But this time I've requested a sleeper jet. You will actually have your own little room where you can sleep, in privacy, the entire flight if you want, with an actual bed."

Reading's eyebrows rose at this little tidbit. "Really?"

"It's good to be rich," said Tommy, as giddy as his girlfriend.

Laura continued. "So, you can arrive well-rested, then we've got air-conditioned vehicles that will take us to the Vietnamese border. You don't even have to get out. This is all for Mai and her reunion with her dad. I've been told you'll get about an hour with him, then we'll head back to Phnom Penh where we have rooms at a five-star hotel reserved, all air-conditioned, I assure you, then we'll head home the next day in the same aircraft."

Acton chuckled as he regarded him. "If you wiggle that ass between air-conditioned venues, you might only have five minutes grand total of exposure to the elements."

Reading sighed. "That's my kind of trip."

Laura smiled at him. "I figured that would make you happy. Of course, if you don't want to go, you have your own suite upstairs that you can stay in until we get back."

He glanced over at the stairs leading to his new haven. It was a tempting idea, though he dismissed it. "No, I'll come with you, just in case you two decide to do something stupid."

Laura held up her hands. "This is a simple two-day trip. We're not even planning on any side-trips."

"Why not?"

"We were lucky to get the visas on compassionate grounds. Trying to tack on additional days would have been too difficult."

Reading cracked his knuckles. "Cambodia isn't exactly Germany. Do we have any security concerns?"

"I don't, but Cameron does. He will be meeting us at the airport with three of his team and some local contacts. They'll provide security while we're there."

Reading had to admit he felt a little better knowing Cameron Leather, former British Special Air Service, would be there with a team. He was excellent at what he did, and the only way Reading would feel any better was if Bravo Team was there, since they'd also have the backing of the US military and intelligence apparatus behind them—Leather was private, so didn't have the fancy toys.

Acton leaned over and fished his cellphone out of his pocket, pulling up a message. His frown went unnoticed by the others as Mai was beyond excited at the prospect of seeing her father, but Reading caught it.

"What's wrong?"

His question had everyone turning to Acton. "Nothing wrong, but I have an interesting email from Professor Chayan Bunthan."

"Who's that?" asked Laura.

"His father was an old friend of Greg's, and his son ended up going to my alma mater, about ten years after I graduated. I met him once, years ago, at his graduation. His father invited Greg and I to attend. Nice kid. Very sharp." Acton scratched his wrist. "I guess he wouldn't be a kid anymore. He's probably early thirties."

"What's he want?" asked Reading, sensing things were about to take a turn.

"He wants me to come to his dig and inspect an artifact he's found."

Laura repositioned on the couch to face her husband. "Where?"

"Thailand."

"Well, that borders Cambodia. We could delay our return and drop by."

"I'm game," said Tommy. "I've always wanted to see Thailand."

Mai elbowed him. "You just want to see the girls."

He grinned. "I already have my own Asian hottie. Why would I want to stare at others?"

"I've seen your browser history."

Reading snorted at Tommy's shocked expression. "Where in Thailand?"

"Outside of some place I've never heard of. Kanchanaburi." Acton tapped away at his phone then pursed his lips. "Huh. Pretty remote." He glanced up at Reading. "I doubt they have air conditioning."

Reading rolled his eyes. "I knew something would ruin this trip."

Laura gave him a look. "Now, now, I see two choices. One, you take the plane home as scheduled, we'll visit the dig site, then come back a couple of days later."

"I like the sound of that."

"Or two, we book you into a fancy hotel in Bangkok, and you can park your butt in front of a TV in an air-conditioned room with an unlimited supply of beer brought to you by buxom Thai beauties."

"Now I like the sound of *that*."

Tommy held up a finger. "Can I stay with him?" Mai swatted him and he laughed. "I was just joking."

"Remember, I've seen your browser history."

Acton looked at Reading. "So, it's settled? You'll stay in Bangkok and we'll head to the dig site. It will probably only be a couple of days. It will give you a chance to unwind from the flight and relax. Who knows, you might even venture outside and see some of the sights."

Reading grunted. "I doubt that, but I think I could stand to relax for a few days and sample the local room service."

"Great. I'll let him know we're coming." Acton began typing a message when he glanced at Laura. "And you better let Leather know to arrange some security in Thailand."

"Why? I thought Thailand was safe."

Acton wagged his phone. "He says to bring security if we can."

Reading tensed, leaning forward. "Does he say why?"

"No, but it is in a remote area. It's probably just a precaution."

Reading leaned back, exhaling slowly. "Maybe I better be coming with you. Just in case."

Khwae Noi Tributary Dig Site
Kanchanaburi District, Thailand

Bunthan turned on his laptop and breathed a sigh of relief as he read Acton's reply to last night's message. He barely knew the man, though his father was friends with him, or at least acquaintances. Acton and his friend, Gregory Milton, had attended his graduation, and both had followed his academic career over the years, and he had followed theirs, especially Acton, who was now fairly famous in the small community of archaeologists.

He was also rich. According to his father, Acton had married money. Huge money. One of the reasons he and his wife were so popular, was that they were extremely generous when it came to funding other projects. According to his father, they traveled by private jet, could be anywhere in the world in a day or two, and provided their own private security to dig sites around the world.

Acton was exactly what he needed.

The moment he showed the artifact to him, he was certain Acton would recognize the problem and would agree to transport it safely to the university in Bangkok. Once there, it would be secure, and there should be nothing else to worry about from the local criminal element.

But his arrival was three days away. The entire camp was abuzz with excitement over the discovery, and he had given strict instructions that no one was to mention it to anyone. No texts, no emails, no social media posts, no photographs. It was too dangerous. He was certain they understood the danger, and the fact every time a motorcycle echoed in the distance put them all on edge, reaffirmed his belief.

Yet it only took one slip-up.

Too many young people today were obsessed with fame. Today you didn't need to be talented to be famous. Before the Internet, you had to be a gifted singer, actor, or artist of some type, to be famous. Now, you just needed a big ass and a willingness to show under-boob while doing a stupid dance to become famous. Today, too many people were famous for being famous. They had no talent.

And he had young men and women here with him that were social media obsessed, some with a following in the tens of thousands just because of the posts they made at the dig sites. He had never minded it in the past, since any attention drawn to the underfunded field, especially in Thailand, would be welcome.

But not when it could put lives at risk.

The jewels alone in the mask were worth millions, and someone like Zhao wouldn't hesitate to kill for it. A mask like they had found could keep him and his men filthy with booze, drugs, and women for the rest of their lives. It would be irresistible if word were to leak.

He eyed the far side of the tent and the tarp covering the floor. He had taken the mask and put it inside a lockbox, then buried it under the floor, telling no one. When asked this morning where it was, he simply told everyone it had been put somewhere safe, and to forget about it.

In three days, Acton would be here with his private security team, and he would give him the mask to take away. In the meantime, everyone simply had to remain quiet, and act as if nothing had happened.

And he had to create a jar that at least had some semblance of jade, for when the students returned.

With Achara.

He leaned back in his chair and sighed, a smile spreading. She was perfect. Everything he could possibly want. She was intelligent, quick-witted, beautiful. Being with her was just…comfortable. After the incident with Zhao, things had calmed down, he had been embraced by her parents, and the rest of the evening had been fantastic. He had walked her home, and the lingering peck on his cheek she gave him had fired his dreams last night, and filled his stray thoughts today.

He was in love.

It was ridiculous to think such a thing. He barely knew her, yet she was all he could think of. She reminded him so much of his late wife, but she was her own woman. They had as many differences as similarities. He loved that she led a simple life and wasn't obsessed with the trappings of modern society, but wasn't scared of them either as she had been educated in the city. By the end of the night, they had spoken of what life would be like married to an archaeology professor that traveled the country, and she had sounded open to it.

Marriage.

He chuckled to himself. The very notion of thinking of such a thing so quickly was absurd. Yet here he was, picturing their wedding day, Achara stunning in her traditional dress, smiling at him with love in her eyes.

He had wondered how someone so beautiful, so captivating, hadn't already been snatched up by some lucky young man, and when he had asked, her mother had shouted the answer.

"She's too picky!"

Achara explained that she found the men of her village too unsophisticated, too uneducated. She wanted intellectual stimulation in a relationship, which was what had attracted her to him.

"So, it wasn't my good looks?"

She had laughed, her cheeks flushing as she looked away. "You're cute too."

A perfect night.

He would be seeing her again tonight, but before he left to see her, he had to fake an artifact well enough to not only fool schoolchildren, but one child's drunken father.

A man who might just kill them all if he thought he was being tricked.

Royal Palace

Ayutthaya, Ayutthaya Kingdom

April 26, 1758

Thammathibet stormed down the wide hallway leading to his father's bedchambers, rage gripping him as the conversation he had just had with Luang replayed over and over in his head. Before he had heard his father wanted Uthumphon to succeed him, he had little interest in the throne. It was a burden he had no desire to take on. However, once Luang had informed him that burden had been taken away from him in this unbelievable betrayal of both family and tradition, he had desired nothing more.

He wanted to be king.

If only to thwart his father's dying wish.

And to prevent his younger brother from having power over him.

They had been good friends growing up, but as they got older, it had become clear that Uthumphon was Father's favorite, but more horrifying, that Uthumphon was more capable. He was smarter, wittier,

61

and far more versed with the inner workings of the kingdom. He spent his days at their father's side, engrossed in all it took to run the realm.

He would make the better king.

But shouldn't that be the eldest son's decision?

If their father had expressed his concerns and asked him to abdicate to his younger brother immediately after becoming king, he might have considered it. In fact, he likely would have eagerly done so. After all, he didn't want to be king, and it would avoid the humiliation he was about to suffer. Everyone in the kingdom would know he had been passed over because he was unworthy. His friends would snicker behind his back, women would find him less appealing, the common folk on the street would no longer cower in fear of what whim of his they might fall victim to.

He would be reduced to the laughingstock of the entire kingdom.

And that had to be stopped.

Two guards blocked his way. "I'm sorry, Your Highness, but there are to be no visitors."

Thammathibet glared at the massive man. "You have the power to block me today, but tomorrow, when I am king, I will have the power to have both your throats slit in front of your families. Let me in or face the consequences."

Both men exchanged nervous glances then stepped aside. Thammathibet opened the door and barged into the room, slamming it shut behind him. His father jerked awake on the bed, his eyes flitting about, searching for the source of the noise when they settled on Thammathibet.

"What are you doing here?"

"I think we have something to discuss, don't you?"

"What are you talking about?"

"Your plan to name Uthumphon king, and not me."

His father frowned. "How did you find out about that?"

"I have friends."

His father grunted. "None that would be privy to that information. Luang told you." He muttered a curse. "I knew the old man was too bound by tradition to heed my wishes."

"Oh, don't worry about that. He intends to make Uthumphon king, just as you asked, but he felt I should be informed so I could perhaps persuade you to change your mind."

His father's eyebrows rose. "Change my mind? Why would I want to do that? And a better question, why do you care? You've never shown any interest in being king. You've shirked your responsibilities from the day you came of age. I would think you'd be relieved that your brother will take on the responsibilities he has clearly shown he has an interest in. You can continue to live your life as you have been, enjoying all the wealth and power you've always had. Your brother will run the kingdom, and everyone will be better for it." He eyed him. "This has nothing to do with wanting to be king, does it? You're upset because you fear the humiliation you think my choice will bring you."

Thammathibet threw his hands in the air. "Of course, I'm upset! How did you think I'd react? I'm to be king. It is tradition, and everyone expects it."

"Even you?"

"Of course, even me."

"Then why have you done nothing to show you're worthy of the position. Being king is an honor, a duty. It is not simply a right. In this kingdom, the king must always be worthy. Fortunately, until now, he who would inherit has always been—"

"Worthy! I know, I know. And I'm not. But I was never given a chance. I never thought you were going to die so young." Thammathibet growled. "This is nonsense! This is so unfair!"

"I'm the one dying before my time. I should think I'd be the one complaining it's unfair."

Thammathibet regarded his father as his chest heaved with indignation. He sighed, his shoulders slumping. "You're right, of course, Father." He dropped on the edge of the bed. "I know we haven't seen eye to eye much over the past several years, and I know I'm the one to blame. This is all my fault, not Uthumphon's, and not yours. I've done this to myself. But once I heard I wasn't to be king, I realized how much I wanted it. I think I can learn to do the job with the help of Uthumphon."

"This isn't a job where there is time to learn. You must be prepared to take over the moment I die. I've been begging you to meet with my advisors so you could be trained, but you have always refused. Your brother has never missed a session."

Thammathibet closed his eyes, inhaling slowly. "But the humiliation."

"Will pass. After a few months, no one will remember, and few will care regardless. Nothing will change in your life, and you know your brother, he will never lord his position over you. Your friends will forget about it, the women will still flock to you, and perhaps in time you will decide you want something more out of life. This is only a humiliation in *your* mind. You can tell your friends that you refused the throne because you wanted to enjoy life, not run a kingdom. They would probably respect you even more."

Thammathibet mulled the idea for a moment. His father was right. He could tell the lie, and his brother would likely back it. It would save him the humiliation, and he'd be a hero in his friends' eyes—the man who would be king, who refused the position so he could enjoy life instead.

It was brilliant.

But there was a better plan, that wouldn't require lying.

"You've always said lying is sinful, and while I haven't practiced what you have preached, I do agree. I believe I have a better solution."

"And what's that?"

"Make me king, then I will immediately abdicate my throne to Uthumphon. That way no one has to lie, tradition is upheld, and you still get what you want."

His father regarded him, his lips pursed as he debated the proposal. It was a good idea, and he was certain his father realized it. It was the only way he could see to save face and avoid the responsibilities that came with sitting on the throne. He did like his father's idea of lying to his friends and telling them he had refused the throne. He would be the hero, though for how long? This lifestyle would eventually become tiresome, and he would want to take a wife and have a family. And what would he say when his children asked him why he wasn't king? Would he tell them that he had turned down the throne because he wanted to party with his friends?

He suppressed a frown. If he were to think of the future, he couldn't refuse the throne if offered. It would be a humiliation for his children yet to be born. And would they lose their right to inherit? This break with tradition had only ever been done in the past when there was no obvious heir. But in this case, it should be him, then his eldest son. His brother should only inherit if there was no male heir. But if his brother became king, would it be *his* eldest son that next became king, and not his own?

This decision could affect a family he didn't yet have in ways he had never considered.

"It is an interesting proposal, my son, but I must refuse it."

Thammathibet's jaw dropped. "Why?"

"I don't think you'll like the answer."

"Of that, I have no doubt, but tell me. I have a right to know."

"I don't trust you."

The jolt to his heart was more than he could have imagined. He and his father didn't get along, but this was the first time anything so horrid had been said directly to him. "You…you don't trust me?"

"Frankly, no. I can't trust that once you have been named king, that you will abdicate to your brother like you said. I fear you will decide to retain power just to spite me and your brother."

"I would do no such thing!"

"And if you did, for the good of the kingdom, there would be only one solution."

Thammathibet's stomach churned, for he feared what that one solution might be.

His father took his hand, giving it a weak squeeze. "We may have our differences, but you are still my son. I love you, even if you hate me. I don't want my family destroyed over this, nor my kingdom. You are all my legacy. Let your brother succeed me without protest, and he will be happy. You will be able to enjoy whatever life you want, and *you* will be happy. And the people will have a leader who wants to lead them, and they will be happy. Please, son, I beg you, don't make this more difficult than it already is."

Thammathibet squeezed his eyes shut, the burn threatening to turn into tears. It was the most heartfelt plea he had ever heard from his father, and it genuinely did move him. Yes, they didn't get along, but he did love his father, and would be heartbroken when he died. He couldn't have the man fearing what would happen to his kingdom and family after he died.

He had to agree to his father's wishes.

There was a knock at the door and Thammathibet rose, wiping his eyes dry with the back of his hand. The door opened and Luang entered carrying a box made of teak, a gold clasp holding the lid in place. It could contain only one thing.

The Mask of Succession.

"Forgive me for intruding, Your Majesty." Luang's eyes darted over to Thammathibet for a moment. "I didn't realize you would have company." He held up the box. "I have brought the Mask of Succession as you requested."

"Thank you, Abbot." The king pointed at a nearby table. "Place it there."

Luang bowed then stepped over to the table, placing the box on it. He unclasped the latch and opened the lid. The man stepped back, staring at the jade mask it contained, adorned with gold and precious jewels. It was priceless in more ways than one, and Thammathibet had always marveled that something so valuable was left in the care of monks and not the palace guard.

He stepped closer, eying the mask. It was mesmerizing, intoxicating, not only for its beauty and opulence, but for what it represented. He who wore it first after the death of the king would become king until his own end.

And he wanted it.

The fact the power was only paces away from him had his chest tight with anticipation, his stomach churning with the unknown it represented. What would it be like to be king? The power, the glory, the respect, the fear? What would it be like to have the power of a living spirit, where his word was law, where any command given had to be obeyed?

Intoxicating, indeed.

"I can see it in your eyes, my son. You would never abdicate to your brother."

Thammathibet continued to stare at the mask before he finally managed to tear his eyes away. "You think so little of me?"

"I fear the temptation will be too great. No man who has ever been offered the mask has refused it. It would take a man of incredible strength of will and integrity of spirit to do such a thing."

"And you believe I possess neither of those traits."

"I believe you possess strength and integrity, but not to the extent required to resist this temptation. Son, I fear even I wouldn't be able to resist if the roles were reversed."

"Yet you expect me to stand idly by while my birthright is stolen from me."

"It is not your birthright. It is only your birthright if you are worthy, and you are not worthy."

Thammathibet's fists clenched and he inhaled sharply, holding his breath before he burst forward and grabbed the mask from its case. Luang gasped in shock, stumbling backward as Thammathibet spun toward his father, fitting the mask over his face and tying it behind his head. "I will be king, Father, and there is nothing you can do about it. It *is* my birthright, and after all the derision directed at me over the years, I deserve it!"

His father stared at him, little emotion on his face. "Wearing the mask before I am dead has no meaning. What do you hope to accomplish with this action?"

"I intend to be king. I should think that would be obvious."

"Then you'll have to kill me, or evade the guards until I'm dead."

Thammathibet drew his blade and Luang gasped yet again before rushing forward and placing himself between the two family members. "Your Highness! You mustn't! He's your father!"

Thammathibet halted his advance and stared at the blade in his hand, his mouth agape at what he had just done. The knife clattered to the ground and he stared at Luang then his father.

And bolted from the room.

Phnom Penh International Airport
Phnom Penh, Cambodia
Present Day

Acton stepped onto the tarmac, the heat radiating off the concrete, and he glanced back at Reading, waiting for the complaint, but none came. Everyone was in a good mood, Mai's bubbly excitement contagious. Even their sometimes-cranky friend wasn't risking ruining this day.

"Hello, professors!"

Acton turned to see their head of security, Cameron Leather, hailing them from the door of the private terminal. Three of his men that Acton recognized were with him, along with four locals. Leather was a former lieutenant colonel in the British SAS, and after retiring, had set up his own private security firm, bringing former Special Forces from around the world under his tent. Laura had required security for her dig in Egypt, and had offered him so much money, that he was now in charge of their personal security whenever needed, and provided permanent security for their digs in Egypt and Peru.

Leather had saved their asses on several occasions, and had even worked in concert with their friends in Bravo Team from time to time. Acton always felt at ease when Leather or one of his men were around, and immediately the tension he hadn't noticed in his shoulders melted away. They were in Cambodia. It wasn't exactly high on his list of countries he would like to be in, and he definitely didn't consider it a place you would let your guard down. The right paperwork, wallet, and connections would deal with the government hassles, and Leather would deal with the local hassles, should they come up.

But they were here for a good time, and while he would keep a wary eye on everything as he even did back home, he would leave the stressing out over their safety to Leather's team, and their good friend Reading, who no doubt was already assessing their situation.

A representative from the charter terminal was already hustling them inside to clear customs as their luggage was unloaded. Laura gave Leather a hug and Acton chuckled at the awkward return then shook the man's hand.

"Good to see you. Anything to report?"

"Smooth so far." Leather held out a hand toward one of the locals. "This is Kosal. He's in charge of the local team. He comes highly recommended by a couple of my men."

Acton shook the man's hand. "Pleasure to meet you."

"Likewise, sir."

Leather continued. "He's been fully briefed. Your travel agent has arranged a helicopter to take us most of the way, then vehicles. The route has been reviewed by Kosal with a couple of minor changes to avoid some known trouble spots. We should be at the border in a few hours."

Laura smiled. "Then we're on schedule. Excellent."

They cleared customs and were soon in a large SUV heading to the heliport with Kosal driving and Leather in the passenger seat. Reading and Acton occupied the middle row with Laura and the kids in the rear.

"Let's get that air conditioning cranked," said Reading as he unbuttoned the top half of his shirt. Leather took care of it and Reading sighed a moment later as they pulled away from the airport, escorted by two other SUVs, front and back.

"So, Mr. Reading, what was it like sleeping in a bed on an airplane?" asked Mai.

Reading twisted in his seat to face her. "Odd at first, but once I fell asleep, I was out like a log." He looked at Laura. "*That* is how I want to travel from now on."

She laughed. "Consider it done."

"Just kidding, of course, though for those long hauls, I definitely wouldn't say no. Over the pond is a waste. By the time you get to sleep, you're already beginning your descent."

"Good point."

Acton leaned forward. "How long until we get to the chopper."

"Fifteen minutes."

Reading frowned. "Is it air-conditioned?"

"If it's not, we'll let you fly on the skid."

Khwae Noi Tributary Dig Site
Kanchanaburi District, Thailand

Bunthan held up his handiwork, his lips pursed. Did it look like jade? No. But in the right light, one might convince the uninformed it was what had been buried in the ground and photographed by a gang leader's daughter. He glanced at Sanun, who had been assisting him all day. "What do you think?"

"Let's hope they're idiots."

"Well, they're children."

"Not all of them are. Your girlfriend—"

"My what?"

Sanun gave him a look. "You're telling me that things didn't go well the past two nights?"

Bunthan's cheeks flushed. "Well, I'm not saying that, no."

"Good. Because you'd be lying. You've had a shit-eating grin for two days. Everyone's noticed."

Bunthan forced a frown. "Am I that transparent?"

"It's good. We're all thrilled to see you so happy. But one of the reasons I believe you're attracted to her is that she is intelligent." Sanun tapped the earthenware jar they had just fired with a makeshift kiln. "*That* will not fool her."

"It doesn't need to."

"So, you told her the truth."

His shoulders sagged. "No."

"Why not? Don't you trust her?"

His eyebrows rose at the question. Did he trust her? He supposed he did, though he barely knew her. If his initial impression of her was accurate, then yes, he did trust her, but people could surprise you, especially when it came to money. But it wasn't trust that had stopped him from telling her the truth. In this case, knowledge was danger. If she knew the truth, and let it slip, or was questioned and caught in a lie, harm might come to her. "I trust her. I just didn't want to put her in any danger."

"Well, you might want to warn her so she doesn't act surprised." Sanun leaned closer, lowering his voice. "Also, it might not be a good precedent to set for your new relationship."

"What do you mean?"

"Well, Professor, you're already lying to her."

He groaned. "You're right, of course. I'm seeing her tonight. I'll tell her what's going on. Professor Acton will be here with his security team tomorrow, then we can rest easy."

If was Sanun's turn to frown. "Do you trust this guy?"

"Implicitly. Surely you've heard of him?"

"I have, but he's American, and thinks he's Indiana Jones."

Bunthan laughed. "I don't think that's a very fair assessment. He's just been caught up in a few things that were beyond his control and handled himself well."

"You need to spend more time on the Internet."

"No thanks."

"I'm serious. If you check this guy out on some of the more fringe sites, you'll find out that he's suspected of being involved in a *lot* of odd goings-on."

"You can't believe everything you read on the Internet."

"No, but if even half of it is true, I think we need to be careful."

Bunthan regarded his prize pupil. "I thought I taught you better than that. Listen to yourself. 'If even half of it is true?' If you go on a conspiracy website filled with lies, do you assume that half of it is true, just because it can't all be lies? I'm quite certain that if he were doing anything nefarious, he'd have been arrested or outed on some credible websites."

Sanun grunted. "I hope you're right, and it's your decision, but I don't trust him."

"At least wait until you meet the man before you condemn him." Bunthan checked his watch and smiled. "I have to get ready. I'm meeting Achara in an hour."

Sanun rose. "Good luck, Professor." He pulled a condom from his pocket and held it out with a grin. "Better take this, just in case it's a really good date."

Bunthan gave him the stink-eye. "I'm a gentleman."

"Yeah, and she's gorgeous." Sanun tossed it onto the table. "Boy Scout's motto." He left the tent, chuckling, and Bunthan eyed the condom.

"Be prepared," he muttered. He grabbed it and put it in a drawer. He wasn't interested in a one-night stand. He was seeking a relationship, and a woman like this wouldn't be looking for sex on a third date.

Would she?

He eyed the drawer, a debate raging.

He growled.

Just get ready!

Cambodia-Vietnam Border

Oyadav, Cambodia

Mai stood by the SUV, impatiently bobbing up and down on her toes as Tommy held her. They had arrived without incident, but if anything were to go wrong, this was where it was going to happen. All the arrangements were informal, based on favors called in and bribes paid. Their contact on the Vietnamese side of the border had confirmed that they were there with Mai's father, but so far no one was being allowed through.

"What's going on?" asked Acton as Leather approached them, Kosal still talking with the border guards.

"They're not cooperating. Normally this is just a formality. Hand over some cash and they let them through on foot. They can meet in no-man's land, then return. But the Cambodians are saying no."

Laura wagged her phone, on a live call with the contact on the other side. "They're good to go on the Vietnamese side. They're just waiting for confirmation from us."

"What's the problem?" asked Acton as Kosal joined them.

Kosal shook his head. "They might have received new orders to not allow these informal reunions, they might have seen a bunch of white people and thought something odd was going on, they could want more money, or they could just be assholes."

Mai rushed over, concern on her face. "Is something wrong?"

Laura put a hand on the young woman's shoulder. "We're not sure yet. It looks like the Cambodians don't want to let you through."

Mai burst into tears and collapsed into Laura's arms, and Acton's heart broke. He pointed at Kosal. "Come with me." He marched over to the guard he had seen Kosal speaking with as Kosal and Leather scrambled to keep up. He stopped in front of the man and pointed at Mai. "That young woman has traveled all the way from America to spend just one hour with her father whom she hasn't seen in years. This may be the last chance she gets." He pulled out a wad of cash from his pocket and grabbed the guard's hand, slapping the money into his palm as Kosal translated. "That's five thousand American dollars." He pulled off his watch that Laura had given them on their first wedding anniversary and held it up. "Rolex. Over twenty-thousand American dollars. It's yours if you give her that hour with her father."

The man's eyes were hidden behind opaque sunglasses, but the twitching on his face suggested indecision. The man squeezed the money in his hand then the other darted out and snatched the watch, stuffing it in his pocket. He raised an arm then shouted something, and the gate was immediately lifted.

"One hour," he said in heavily accented English.

Acton smiled. "Thank you, sir." He turned and waved at Mai. "Let's go, kiddo! You've got one hour!"

Mai squealed in glee as she rushed toward him, Laura already talking to the other side. Mai slammed into his arms, giving him a hug and a big kiss on the cheek. "Thank you so much!"

He pointed at the gate opening on the other side and she screamed at the sight of a man who appeared far older than his years should allow, limping toward her with a cane. She rushed past the gate and along the road, and Acton bit down on his finger as Mai's father held his arms out, embracing his daughter for the first time in years.

It was times like these that he truly appreciated what could be accomplished when enough money was at hand. If he were still a lowly professor, none of this would have been possible, but thanks to Laura's late brother, they could do things like this and bring joy into broken hearts.

He rejoined the others and Laura hugged him, tears flowing freely down her cheeks. He held out a hand and Reading clasped it, pumping it hard, his own eyes glistening as Tommy struggled to maintain control.

"What did it finally take to convince him?" asked Reading.

"Five grand and my Rolex."

Laura looked up at him. "The one I gave you for our anniversary?"

"I figured you wouldn't mind."

She smiled and rested her head on his chest. "It went to a good cause. I'll get you a new one."

Tommy's jaw dropped. "Five grand wasn't enough, but a watch was?"

Reading chuckled. "Son, that Rolex was probably worth ten thousand dollars."

"Try twenty," corrected Acton.

"Actually, it was around thirty," said Laura.

Acton pushed her away. "You spent thirty grand on a watch!"

"Nothing is too good for my baby."

Acton rolled his eyes at Reading. "I'm a kept man."

She squeezed his butt. "And you like it."

He laughed and hugged her hard, then they all stood and watched as Mai and her father enjoyed their reunion, seeing each other for what might be the last time, and he thought of what he would give to see his mother one last time, even if it were just for an hour.

Some cash and a watch were a small price to pay for the joy they were witnessing.

Muban Chong Sadao

Kanchanaburi District, Thailand

"I have to tell you something, and it might make you mad."

Achara recoiled slightly from Bunthan. "What?"

He could hear the trepidation in her voice, and it had him queasy. "I lied to you."

Her eyes widened. "About what?"

"About what Zhao's daughter found."

Her shoulders slumped in relief. "My God! I thought it was about something serious." She giggled. "Of course you lied, I'm no fool."

He stared at her, shocked. "Wait, you knew?"

She laughed. "It was so obviously jade that she found. You had to lie to him, otherwise he'd be down there tearing apart your dig site looking for it and any more that might be hidden there. You don't have to apologize to me."

He sighed, taking her hand. "You are so amazing. No wonder I…" He wanted to say it, he wanted to tell her that he loved her, but it was too soon. Far too soon. He'd terrify the poor woman. He instead smiled. "You're perfect."

She looked away, gripping his hand. "I'm far from, but I'm clever enough to play along with your little fiction." She faced him. "So, tomorrow, when we return to the dig, I'm to play along with your forgery?"

He reached into the back of the van and retrieved the vase he and Sanun had worked on. He handed it to her. "This is what we've come up with."

She held it up in the fading light, running her fingers gently across the smooth surface. "Impressive. It certainly matches what you described last night, and it should fool Zhao and the students."

"You think so?"

She handed it back to him. "I certainly hope so. If it doesn't…"

He returned the vase to the back. "If it doesn't, do you think he might become violent?"

She shivered. "If he thinks there is jade or something else valuable there, he's the type that would kill you all to have it."

He stared out the windshield, sweat trickling down his back at her words. It was exactly what he had already been thinking, but for her to confirm his fears made everything too real.

"What's wrong?"

He decided he had to trust her. "I haven't told you what we actually did find."

En Route to Phnom Penh, Cambodia

Mai continued to weep in the rear row as Tommy and Laura attempted to console her. Acton watched, smiling gently at her as his own chest ached with the pain she must be feeling. Her wails had settled into whimpers, and part of him wondered if this had been a wise move. Until today, she had resigned herself to never seeing her father again. Now she had seen him, and from what she had gasped out, some of her worst fears had been realized.

He wasn't well.

It sounded like diabetes and blood pressure issues, plus he had taken a nasty fall, hence the cane. He had been hiding these things from her in their rare communiques, but now they knew.

And they could do something about it.

He reached out and took her hand, and she stared up at him, her eyes red. "Listen, now that we know what's wrong, we can help."

"H-How?"

"We'll use the same contacts we just used."

Laura agreed. "Yes, this was an experiment. Now that we know it can work, we can make this an annual event if you want. Semi-annual. Whatever. This won't be the last time you see him. And with our newly established contacts, we can get him money, medicine, whatever he needs."

Mai stared at Laura, her face brightening slightly. "Do you really think you can help him?"

"Yes, I don't see why not. The problem has been getting things to him, because of your situation. We could never send him money directly, and we couldn't risk sending anything to his friends or other family members because if they were caught, they could get in trouble. But this new conduit we've set up doesn't have that problem. We simply wire transfer the money, and they drop it off. From now on, we should be able to make sure he has everything he needs."

Mai leaned against Laura, blowing her nose yet again. "Oh, thank God for you two. I don't know what I'd do without you. I owe you so much."

Acton squeezed her hand. "We're the ones who owe you. You saved us, remember? If it weren't for you, we'd be rotting in a prison cell in Vietnam."

"Or we'd be dead," said Laura.

"So, we owe you. I say we make this a regular thing. At least once a year if not twice, but first we get the money flowing and get your father's health taken care of."

She sniffed and smiled. "Thank you."

85

Laura patted her hand. "Think nothing of it. Now, tell us everything."

Mai eagerly relayed all the news from home, her tears and fears forgotten for the moment, but eventually her adrenaline ran out and she was snoozing against Tommy's shoulder, a smile on her face.

Acton reached out and touched Laura's cheek. "You did a good thing today."

She smiled, her eyes glistening. "It was special, wasn't it?"

"Absolutely."

Reading checked his usually booming voice. "These contacts you made, who are they?"

She nodded at Leather in the passenger seat. "A combination of friends of Cameron's and some contacts of our travel agent, Mary."

Reading shook his head. "Just who the hell is she? She seems to be able to arrange anything anywhere at any time."

"I asked her that once, and she said I didn't want to know."

Acton's eyes widened slightly. "That sounds ominous."

"That's what I thought. I got the impression she used to be some sort of Moneypenny in the British government."

"Big step down from that to a travel agent."

Laura shrugged. "She's not just any travel agent."

Reading grunted. "Clearly."

"When my brother died, she reached out to me and offered her services, the same services she used to perform for him. She basically described herself as the provider of the impossible. Whatever I needed, just let her know, and she'd arrange it. I mostly used her for my travel arrangements, but over the years she's proven very useful in getting me information, visas, whatever, so I thought I'd give this a shot, and she came through."

Acton chewed his cheek. "I'd love to have Kane run her name and see what came up."

Laura gave him a look. "Don't you dare! The last thing we need is her dumping us because we've upset her. We'll never be able to replace her."

Reading agreed. "Definitely keep her happy. She's worth her weight in gold, that one."

Acton held up his hands in defeat. "Fine, fine, I won't ask him." He grinned. "Besides, it's more fun to speculate. Moneypenny, hey?"

Laura wagged a finger at him. "Stop that, or you're liable to call her that on the phone the next time you talk to her."

He glanced at his watch then cursed, rubbing the empty wrist. "I can't wait to get to the hotel. I'm exhausted. Not all of us got a cushy bed to sleep in last night."

Reading grinned.

Kosal glanced in the rearview mirror. "When we get to the hotel, we'll be leaving a team on your floor and in the lobby. It's already been arranged with hotel security. Tomorrow morning, we'll transport you to the airport so you can catch your flight to Bangkok."

Leather twisted in his seat. "I've already arranged for us to be met at the airport by a local team, and we'll set out directly for the dig site. It's quite the drive." He smiled at Reading. "You're going to love it."

Reading groaned. "Can't we just take a helicopter in?"

Leather shook his head. "Sorry, mate, but the canopy is too thick to get anywhere near the dig, and we can't exactly land in the middle of a village if we're trying to keep a low profile."

"*Are* we trying to keep a low profile?" asked Acton.

"I always try to, despite both your efforts to thwart me at every turn."

Acton flashed a grin at Laura, who apologized for them both. "But you think there could be trouble?"

"It isn't a great area. Very poor, and the government has very little presence. My main concern is that your friend found something, wouldn't say what it was, and suggested you bring security. That's enough red flags for me to want to get in and out as quickly as possible."

"We were planning on spending a couple of days there," said Acton. "And besides, by the time we get there, it will probably be too late to turn around and head back."

"It's never too late to leave a danger zone. I'll leave it up to you, but my recommendation is we get there, assess and secure the area, you conduct your business, then we leave. We've got extra lighting on the vehicles we've arranged, spare tires, emergency equipment, and GPS. It might be a slower return trip, but the more miles we put between us and that dig site before anyone finds out we were there, the better."

"Well, let's play it by ear. I'd hate to just show up then leave. I'd like to see the dig and get to know Chayan a little bit better in person." He held up a finger to cut off Leather's concerns. "*However,* if you deem it too dangerous, then we'll leave right away. Agreed?"

Leather acquiesced. "You're the client."

Reading grunted. "How many times have you said that before one of them got their asses in a bind?"

Leather chuckled. "Too many times to count."

Royal Palace

Ayutthaya, Ayutthaya Kingdom

April 26, 1758

Thammathibet sprinted out the grand doors leading from the palace, his personal guard bowing deeply, clearly startled to see him wearing the mask. It was merely ceremonial, worn only after the king's death in front of witnesses, and at the coronation. Outside of that, it was never seen, yet here he wore it as if to a costume party.

"The king is dead! I am now your king!" he shouted as he raced past them, heading for the main gate. His guard followed, several catching up and passing him to clear the way. He glanced over his shoulder at the doors to the palace, yet they remained as he had left them, and there was no sign of pursuit.

They must still be debating what to do.

It made sense. He had stolen the mask, something his father could never have expected, and he must be deciding what orders to give. Any other thief would be hunted down and executed, but when the son of the king does something like this, a different response was demanded.

He wondered what that response would be.

He approached the gates and the startled guards stared at him, slack-jawed. "Open the gate in the name of your king!"

They continued to stare and the head of his guard, Taeng, roared at them. "You heard your king!"

The men scrambled and the gates swung open. Thammathibet burst through as a horn sounded behind them, the coded pattern indicating the palace grounds should be secured.

He paid it no mind.

He came to a halt at the bottom of the winding road leading up to the gate, struggling to catch his breath as his guards spread out.

Taeng approached. "Your Highness, I mean, Your Majesty, what is happening?"

It was a question he had anticipated, and in the short race from his father's bedchambers to here, he could come up with only one explanation that would fit his actions. "The king is dead. The mask was placed on my head by the senior abbot as is tradition, but my brother objected and his private guard attacked. I escaped, but I fear he has corrupted my father's guard, and they now serve my brother. We must find a safe haven outside of the city so we can gather our forces and those loyal to tradition, and take control of my kingdom."

Taeng's head slowly shook through the entire explanation. "This is incredible, Your Majesty. I cannot believe the king's personal guard would turn on you. From the moment you were given the mask, you became their king. It is inconceivable that they would back your brother."

"He must have corrupted them somehow. Whatever the explanation is, it does not matter. Send a man to gather my friends. Tell them what has happened and that we will need help. Tell them to spread the word throughout the city that the king is dead, and that I have been named king and wear the mask. I want everyone to know who now rules them, so they will rally to my side."

"Where will we go?"

"South. It is the closest gate. Once outside, if we make it to the bridge, we can easily hold them off long enough for my brother to come to his senses. He's mad with grief, and I am certain can be made to see this course he has set upon isn't what father would have wanted."

"Very well, Your Majesty." Taeng stepped away, executing the orders, and several of the guards sprinted in different directions, the rest forming up around their new king. "We are ready, Your Majesty. We should get moving."

Thammathibet nodded and they began a quick jog toward the southern gate as horns continued to sound from the palace, their call repeated throughout the city. Taeng frowned as he glanced over his shoulder at Thammathibet. "Your Majesty, they just called for the city to be sealed."

Thammathibet cursed. "My brother is clever." Guilt racked him as he continued to tarnish his brother's good name. If there were anyone in this kingdom who wouldn't do any of the things he now accused him of, it was his brother. "What will the guard do?"

"They will obey their king if they know what's good for them!"

Thammathibet smiled slightly from behind the mask. They rounded a bend, the mighty southern gates just ahead. They slowly closed, those traveling the road into and out of the city rushing toward it before they were blocked by the heavy doors, though thwarted by a line of guards holding back those on either side.

"Halt, in the name of the king!" shouted Taeng as he sprinted ahead, Thammathibet's guard spreading out in a wedge in front of him, an arrowhead of muscle and sword parting the crowds.

The guards at the gate turned to see what the commotion was about, the doors momentarily pausing. "Who goes there?"

"Taeng, head of the king's personal guard!"

"You aren't the head of the king's personal guard. Sangkhit is!" challenged the man in charge of the gate. He signaled for the others to continue closing it.

"The king is dead! Prince Thammathibet is now our king, and I am the head of his guard! Open those gates at once!"

Everyone stared, soldier and civilian alike, the news that their king was dead no doubt shocking. The gates once again halted their inexorable close as the wedge continued forward through the crowd as it scurried out of the way.

"Why haven't we been informed?" asked the guard.

"Do you want the king to personally inform everyone in his kingdom that he has assumed the throne after his father's death? Are you somehow special, that you deserve to be informed personally?"

The guard appeared flustered and took a step back as Taeng reached the gates. The wedge pushed through and the guard gasped at the sight of Thammathibet, wearing the mask no doubt only ever described to those gathered, for all were commoners who would never have had an opportunity to see it before today.

And they bowed.

Every single one of them, including the guards that had challenged them.

It sent a shiver throughout his entire body and affirmed his rash decision. He wanted this. He wanted this power, this adulation. This was what he was born to do.

And there was no way he was letting his father deprive him of that.

Khwae Noi Tributary Dig Site

Kanchanaburi District, Thailand

Present Day

Achara stared at the mask, her mouth agape, her eyes bulging. "It's beautiful!" she hissed, and he put a finger to his mouth, urging her to keep quiet. "Sorry," she whispered.

"It's all right. Everyone here knows about it, so I guess it's fine. I've just been on edge so much since we found this."

She gently returned the mask to its box. "You do know what that is, don't you?"

He eyed her with a slight smirk. "I suspect I do, but what do you think it is?"

"It's obviously the Mask of Succession."

He smiled. "That's exactly what I think it is, but how did it get here?"

"Well, that's rather obvious if you know the area."

He eyed her. "What do you mean? History tells us it was somehow lost during Uthumphon's succession to the throne. Other than that, no one knows."

She wagged a finger at him. "Sometimes you professors rely too much on books. You need to get your hands dirty and talk to the elders, listen to their stories, to the folklore. Around here, the story is well known, though dismissed as just a story." She tapped the box. "Now that you've found it, it lends credence to the oral history."

"And what is that oral history?"

"In a nutshell, it was lost during a spat between two princes competing for the throne. It was lost over a bridge that led to the capital city of the Ayutthaya Kingdom, and was swept downriver and found by a fisherman. When the kingdom collapsed, he fled and settled here."

"I think there are a lot of holes in that story."

She eyed him. "You do know where my people come from, don't you?"

He shook his head. "I'm afraid I haven't had time to research the area very much."

"We're from central Thailand, south of the former capital of Ayutthaya. The oral history tells that we fled the fall, so the timing works, and obviously, since you've found the mask, the stories must be true."

Bunthan stared at her for a moment, more infatuated now than just a minute before. The idea of collaborating with her on this was exciting, intoxicating. "Can you take me to one of these elders who knows the full story?"

"Absolutely. If you like, we can meet one of them tonight."

"That would be fantastic!"

"Excellent. It's my grandmother. She's been dying to meet you."

He laughed. "So, under the spotlight once again."

"This is what happens when you court a woman from a small town. Everyone in the family wants to express their opinion on your worthiness."

"How am I doing so far?"

She leaned in close, staring into his eyes. "I think you're doing wonderfully."

A motorcycle engine revved in the distance and Bunthan jerked to his feet, quickly closing the metal box containing the mask, then returning it to its hiding place under the tarpaulin floor of the tent. He placed a hand on his chest, shaking his head. "I'm sorry. We can't be too careful."

"This American you told me about. Can you trust him?"

"Absolutely, though I'm not sure if he will be willing. I didn't tell him what was going on. I'm just relying on his good nature and what I know about him to take the mask out of here and safely to the university."

"That's asking a lot, don't you think?"

He sighed. "It is, and I feel guilty about it, but I don't see what choice I have. He's bringing a security team, so the risk should be minimal. For us, however, it is too great. We have no weapons, no way of defending ourselves. If Zhao decides to come here, we're in serious trouble." He paused. "Maybe we should wait to talk to your grandmother. Once it's out of here, then it's fine if people find out. Until then, I think it's best we keep things quiet."

Achara agreed then stepped forward, wrapping her arms around him and burying her head in his chest. He embraced her, his heart hammering as he breathed in her scent, closing his eyes as he imagined much more. "I'll be so happy when this is all over. I didn't realize what you were going through. You must be so stressed."

"You have no idea. All these people here are my responsibility. If something were to happen to them…"

She patted his chest and stared up at him. "Everything will be fine, I'm sure. Hopefully your friend can help."

"Hopefully."

She pushed away gently. "I have to go. School starts in half an hour and I can't be late. I'll see you this evening?"

"Seven o'clock. I can't wait."

She leaned in and gave him a soft kiss on the lips and his knees nearly gave out. "I'll see you soon," she whispered, then turned and left the tent, her scooter firing up and whining out of the dig site and onto the road.

He collapsed in his chair and stared up at the heavens, thanking the spirits for bringing her into his life.

I'm going to marry that woman.

En Route to Khwae Noi Tributary Dig Site
Kanchanaburi District, Thailand

Acton gripped the handhold over his head as they hit another rut, grinning at Tommy as Reading erupted with another string of curses, only half of which he understood. The journey had begun smooth, but the farther from Bangkok they traveled, the worse the roads became. Their local contact, a man named Vidura, assured them he had built the road conditions into his time estimate, and if Tommy's monitoring on his tablet were any indication, the man was telling the truth.

But the rough ride made it seem longer, and he felt for his aging friend. Gallivanting off on trips like these were for the young, or at least the younger. Five years ago, their friend would have kept up better, but he had taken a turn for the worse over the past few years. Reading was convinced his desk job at Interpol was responsible, and it was definitely a possibility, though Acton feared something more serious might be going on.

Yet bringing up Reading's health in front of the man always resulted in an argument. About the only one who could ever get through to him was Laura, so he left these things in her hands. Acton had noticed her concerned glances at their friend during this trip, and he would talk with her when they were back home about sitting Reading down for a heart-to-heart.

Blood tests could identify something that could be treated, something that might turn his life around and bring back the friend they once knew. Yet it could all still be old age. Acton didn't consider Reading old by any means, but as the years piled on, so did the damage. Reading could walk all over Europe with them, enjoy himself in Spain or London, but throw him into an environment like this, and it seemed he just couldn't take it.

It was a mistake to have brought him, though there was no turning back now, however Acton had made a decision. They were not staying for two days. They would absolutely return tomorrow, and perhaps even tonight, depending on how Reading was feeling. Sleeping on a cot in a tent might be more comfortable than enduring another eight hours of these roads.

"We're almost there," announced Vidura, pointing at a small town ahead. "This is the muban of Chong Sadao. About the only civilization near the dig site. This would be where your friends would pick up their supplies and enjoy a meal. Simple folk and normally friendly."

"Muban?" asked Tommy.

"Village."

Acton smiled at a group of children playing along the road who had stopped to stare at the small convoy. One waved and he returned it as a beautiful young woman rushed over to herd them toward a rusted-out school bus. He wondered if she were their schoolteacher, and where they might be off to. He checked his watch and frowned at the bare wrist. He peered ahead at the dash to see the time. It was nearing the end of the school day, so perhaps it was just to return them home, though he would think in a place this size, most would walk. They cleared the town in minutes and were soon on a winding road that hugged what appeared to have once been a reasonably sized river.

"What's the story here?" asked Laura as she leaned across for a look.

"A hydroelectric project upstream has the river down to a trickle compared to before," explained Vidura. "I did a little looking into your professor friend's project, and apparently a lot of things that had been buried over the years are being found. I guess it has all you types excited."

Acton chuckled. "Yeah, it doesn't take much." He too had taken some time last night to read up on the dig site, and was eager to see what had been uncovered. It was a wonderful opportunity to see how these people lived over two hundred years ago, barely touched by the outside world. The village, preserved by the mud that had buried it, could provide them with valuable insights into the daily lives of these people, similar to what had been revealed in other calamitous findings such as Pompeii.

"We're here," said Vidura as he followed the lead vehicle and turned off the road and into a small encampment. They came to a stop and everyone climbed out, Reading stretching loudly before swatting at a fly.

"Professor Acton!"

Acton turned to see Bunthan emerge from a large tent, smiling broadly as his team gathered around. "Chayan! So good to see you again after all these years." He shook the man's hand then made the introductions as Leather's team spread out, securing the area and no doubt assessing their surroundings.

Bunthan shook Laura's hand. "A pleasure, Professor. I've of course followed your work over the years, along with your husband's. Very impressive, both of you."

She smiled. "Thank you. And I've done some reading on you. It looks like you're making quite the name for yourself as well."

Reading swatted again, muttering something Disney would disapprove of. Bunthan flagged down one of his students. "Get Mr. Reading some mosquito netting, would you?"

The student disappeared and returned a moment later with a hat equipped with a net. Reading thanked the man and donned it, pulling the net down around his neck.

"Better?"

Reading nodded. "Much, thank you. Do you have an air conditioner?"

Acton laughed and slapped his friend on the back. "You can sit in the car if you want."

Reading shook his head. "Bollocks to that. I'm here, so I might as well see what there is to see."

Bunthan gave them a quick tour of the site, Acton and Laura both pleased to see standard practices followed despite the obviously low budget.

"How is your funding?" asked Acton.

Bunthan sighed. "Abysmal, as per usual." He waved a hand at the area. "We can manage with our numbers, but the working conditions are terrible. We have a small diesel generator that we use to charge up our devices and batteries once a day, and those keep our lights going and our big extravagance, the Starlink system."

Laura squeezed Acton's hand. "What do you need?"

"What do you mean?"

"If money were no object, what would you need?"

Bunthan chuckled. "Well, nicer tents, a portable air conditioner for the community tent, a better kitchen with more food. A bigger generator. The list is as long as my arm, and my funding about the length of my pinky."

Acton laughed. "I'll tell you what. You put together a list, prioritized into need, want, and nice to have, and we'll see what we can do."

Bunthan stared at them both, his mouth agape. His jaw snapped shut. "I didn't invite you out here for that, please believe me."

Laura reached out and patted his arm. "We know you didn't, but we have been very fortunate in our lives, and would like to help." She waved a hand at the site. "This appears to be a worthy project. I can't wait to read the papers that come out of it, and if we can help make things more comfortable and more productive, then we're happy to help."

Bunthan's head slowly shook as he smiled at them both. "You have no idea how happy that makes me. I swear, you won't regret it. I'll put together the list tonight, if it doesn't seem too greedy."

"Not at all. The sooner we have it, the sooner we can act on it."

A horn honked and they all turned to see the beat-up school bus they had passed earlier come to a stop on the road, a dozen children erupting from it a moment later followed by the same beautiful young woman.

Acton noticed Bunthan's face light up, and he was certain it had nothing to do with the children. "Friend of yours?" he asked.

Bunthan flushed. "As a matter of fact, yes."

"She's lovely," said Laura.

"She is that." Bunthan sighed. "You, umm, of course heard about my wife?"

Acton frowned. "Yes, Greg told me. I did send you my condolences—"

Bunthan cut him off. "Yes, of course you did, I'm sorry I forgot. It was so overwhelming, I simply couldn't reply to them all."

"No apology necessary." Acton took Laura's hand. "What is this young lady's name?"

"Achara Panya. She's the local schoolteacher. Very bright. Very sweet. Very…"

"Very beautiful," finished Laura. "I think you two make a lovely couple."

Bunthan shifted uncomfortably. "Well, it's only been a few days. I'm not sure if you could call us a couple yet."

Acton winked at Laura. "If the smile she has on is any indication, I'd say you're definitely a couple. That woman is happy to see you, let me tell you." He held out a hand. "Why don't you introduce us?"

Bunthan eagerly agreed and they walked over to meet the arriving students and their teacher, along with another young woman. "Miss Panya and Miss Photsi, these are fellow archaeologists, Professors Acton and Palmer, and their friends Mr. Reading, Mr. Granger, and Miss Trinh."

Handshakes all around were followed by Achara awkwardly keeping a respectful distance from Bunthan, though there was little doubt to the adults in the vicinity that there was chemistry at play. Bunthan spoke first, turning to the children, all appearing to be in the tween age group. He said something to them, and they all responded excitedly.

Achara stepped closer and explained. "The last time we were here, they found, umm, something, in the mud. The professor promised he would have it cleaned up for the next time they came. They're very eager to see what it is they found."

"They are definitely very excited," laughed Laura. "Your English is excellent, by the way."

Achara flushed slightly. "Thank you. My parents sent me away to learn in the city when I was younger. They wanted me to have better opportunities than they had, but I came back." She shrugged. "I guess I missed home too much, but I also wanted to teach the children here what I had learned. This area is so poor, education is too often

105

neglected, and these children end up being put to work to help their families. My dream is to one day get my people to realize how important it is to keep them in school so they can compete in the modern world."

"A laudable goal," said Reading. "I wish you luck."

"We all do," agreed Acton. "We'll talk later about perhaps setting up some sort of scholarship fund."

Achara's eyes widened. "You would do that?"

Laura smiled, rubbing the young woman's upper arm. "Anything we can do to help."

Acton stepped back as the children rushed toward the large tent. Photsi snapped something and they came to an abrupt halt at the edge of the netting. Bunthan disappeared inside then reemerged a moment later, holding up a medium-sized jar, fired in green glaze. Acton's eyes narrowed slightly. "That's remarkably well preserved to have been found in the mud," he murmured.

Laura agreed. "I was thinking the same thing. It should be dull. That could have been fired this morning."

Achara leaned in, her voice barely a whisper. "It was, but you mustn't let on, otherwise we could be in danger."

Reading stepped closer. "Did she say we could be in danger?"

Acton nodded. "I think we're going to need a better explanation."

"It will have to wait," said Achara. "Please, don't say anything. I thought Professor Bunthan would have explained everything to you, but I guess there was no time. It's essential the children leave here thinking this is what they found the other day. No one in town can know about the mask."

Acton turned to her, his eyes narrowing. "Mask?"

She shook her head. "Please."

Acton frowned but said nothing, the woman clearly scared. Bunthan held up the jar, no doubt explaining in Thai the so-called history surrounding it, much to the delight of the children. A couple of them had cellphones and were snapping pictures of it, and Achara cringed.

"What's wrong?" asked Laura.

"One of the girls, Dara, has a phone. If her father sees the photos…"

"What?"

"There could be trouble. He saw the jade in the photo from two days ago. That jar may be green, but it is obviously not jade. He won't be fooled."

Reading stepped closer, surveying their surroundings, paying particular attention to the road. "And if he's not fooled?"

"He could come here with his gang to steal the mask."

"What mask?" asked Laura.

"The Mask of Succession."

Acton's eyes widened and Laura gasped. Achara implored them with bulging eyes to control themselves, and Acton shielded his face with a hand. "Are you certain?"

"Yes. Professor Bunthan showed it to me this morning. There can be no doubt. If word gets out, Zhao's gang will set upon this place."

"And Zhao is the girl's father?"

107

"Yes."

Reading exhaled loudly. "When will he see her?"

"She lives with her mother, but he's showing an interest. He might see her after school, tonight, tomorrow, I don't know. But if he sees the photos she's taken, depending on how drunk he is, he'll be asking questions."

"Does the town have Internet?" asked Tommy.

Achara nodded. "A few of the businesses do, and have wi-fi set up so people can have access. Plus, we have cellular access. It's not great, and it's spotty at times, of course, but we do have access."

Tommy pulled out his phone and began doing something as Reading flagged Leather. The former operator jogged over.

"What's up?"

"Possible trouble," replied Reading as he took him aside to explain the situation.

Tommy cursed.

"What is it?" asked Acton, his chest tightening.

"They've got Internet *here*."

"So?"

"So, they've got it set up with no security. Anyone can connect."

Acton's head whipped toward the children, at least three cellphones in sight. "You don't mean—"

"If they're accustomed to free wi-fi being available in their town, then they probably have their phones set to connect to any available network. Those photos they're taking—"

"Are already in the cloud," gasped Mai.

Achara's hand darted to her mouth. "Then he might already know!"

Muban Chong Sadao

Kanchanaburi District, Thailand

Zhao leaned against his motorcycle, taking another swig of his beer. It was mid-afternoon and he was comfortably numb already, which suggested the evening could turn out to be a fun one. Yet he had held back. In fact, he had all of his men holding back.

Three beer limit until he knew the truth.

In the light of day, he had reexamined the photo his daughter had taken, and to him it was jade, not some glass concoction like that fancy city professor had said. But he couldn't be certain. He was no expert, and had only seen jade a couple of times in his life, and always from a distance. He just knew it was worth money, perhaps a lot of money if it were some ancient artifact. He knew little of these things, but knew enough to know that if his daughter had discovered something made from jade at some dig site, then not only was it probably worth more than he could imagine, she should own it.

Which meant *he* should own it.

His phone pinged and he brought up his daughter's cloud storage. He stared at the new photos that had just been uploaded of the jar the professor had been talking about. It was definitely green, but it wasn't jade.

There was no way it could ever be mistaken for jade.

He handed the phone to his second-in-command and best friend, Chula. "Does that look like jade to you?"

Chula peered at the phone then shook his head, passing it along. "No way, boss. That's just glass." The rest agreed before the phone finally made it back to Zhao.

He growled. "That bastard lied to me." He headed into their clubhouse. "Let's teach those big city assholes that you don't steal from little girls."

Khwae Noi Tributary Dig Site

Kanchanaburi District, Thailand

Acton walked over to join Reading and Leather, along with Vidura, as one of the SUVs pulled up onto the road, leaving the site. "What's going on, gentlemen?"

Leather pointed at the road. "Apparently, the only way out is through the town. The other way dead-ends a couple of klicks west of here."

Acton jutted his chin toward the departing vehicle. "Where are they going?"

"To set up a checkpoint, just in case," explained Vidura.

"Can we do that?"

Vidura shrugged. "Technically, no, but they'll only stop any trouble that's trying to come here."

"Do you think we're in danger?"

"If the local gangs think there is something valuable here, then yes."

"Then what do you recommend?"

"We get the hell out of here ASAP," said Leather. "This is exactly what I was fearing could happen. He lured you here, Professor. He knew there was possible danger, otherwise he wouldn't have made that fake jar."

Acton had to agree, and at the moment wasn't at all pleased with Bunthan. If he had just told them the truth from the get-go, they could have done things differently. Certainly Tommy, Mai, and Reading wouldn't be here, nor Laura if he could have convinced her. Hell, *he* might not even be here. They could have arranged for secure transport through Leather, and left this all to the pros.

But instead, they were all here under false pretenses, and potentially in danger.

Yet the milk was already spilled.

"Plan?" he asked.

"That depends. Are we taking the mask with us?" asked Leather.

"I don't see that we have a choice. If we leave it here, then these people are all in danger. If we take it with us, then make it known, they should leave this place alone, though I would suggest they all leave at least until things cool down."

"We don't have the resources to evacuate this many people. It looks like they only have one van. It can't carry all of them, and we're pretty full up."

"What about the children?" Reading pointed at them, still gathered around Bunthan. "We can't just leave them."

"Actually, they're the one group we could probably leave here."

Reading stared at Leather, flabbergasted. "Are you mad?"

"They're local children. One of them is the daughter of one of the gang members. We could probably just leave them here with their teacher, and they'll be fine. Better yet, get them on that bus right now, and send them home before the trouble starts."

"I think I prefer that idea," said Acton, having had the same reaction as Reading.

A motorcycle engine whined in the distance, joined by several others, and a string of curses erupted from them all.

"What the hell do we do now?"

Approaching Khwae Noi Tributary Dig Site
Kanchanaburi District, Thailand

Zhao gunned it around a bend in the road leading to the big city professor's camp, the cold steel pressed against his back giving him the courage to face whatever might lie ahead. He had surveyed the camp a couple of times, and it was just academic types—no weapons, no guards.

Too trusting.

Out here in the jungle, away from the city, it was every man for himself. At least that was how he had led his life. His father had been the same. Brutal. He beat him for every sideways glance, and his mother always had a black eye or worse.

Until the day his father had killed her in a drunken rage.

That was the day Zhao took his father's gun and shot him six times. The authorities had been called and he was taken to a police station in the city then handed over to monks who ran an orphanage. He lasted one night before he ran away and made his way back home, living on the streets he had grown up on, and making his name.

Now he was feared, just like his father was, yet he never beat any woman he was with unless they got in his way. He had a feeling Achara would receive a good walloping before the day was through. She had participated in the lie, and she was the professor's weak point. He clearly had feelings for her, the two of them parading around town like teenagers in the city.

It was disgusting.

He had always thought his daughter's teacher was decorous, but she had lost all sense of morality the moment that man had arrived in town. They'd both be taught a lesson before the night was through, and perhaps Achara, too good for any local man, might be introduced to the pleasures of the flesh in front of her lover should they not cooperate.

Something had been found, something so valuable it was not only worth lying over, but also going to all the trouble to make a fake green glass jar. If it had just been a shard of jade, broken off years ago, then it wouldn't be worth going to such extremes. That meant it was much bigger, and valuable.

Incredibly valuable.

It didn't take much to live well in these parts. If he could find what it was and sell it, he'd live like a king for the rest of his life. His heart pumped hard at the thought, then ran into overdrive when he squeezed hard on the brake after spotting what was around the bend.

A roadblock.

An SUV blocked the road and five men stood behind it, three Thai, two whites, all with guns. He wasn't expecting this. When had these people arrived? They hadn't been here the other day, and there was only one road leading here. He cursed. They must have arrived when he was still sleeping off last night's party.

He turned to Chula as he came to a halt beside him. "Go back to town. Put the word out. I want everybody down here, now. Armed. Guns, machetes, Molotov cocktails. Anything they can find. If they have armed guards, then whatever they found must be worth millions."

Chula's eyes flared at the amount then he gunned his engine, spinning around and racing back to bring reinforcements.

Zhao stood. "What's going on here? We have a right to pass!"

One of the Thais replied. "You can come through, but no weapons."

"We don't have weapons."

"Then you'll be allowed to pass. Advance one at a time, and you'll be searched."

"You aren't government. You have no right to search us."

The man shrugged. "If you want to pass, you'll be searched. You can complain to the government later if you want."

Zhao whipped out his weapon, aiming it at them, and immediately he had five much more impressive weapons aimed at him. "My daughter is down there! I demand she be brought to me!"

"Sir, put down the weapon!"

"Boss!" hissed one of his men, clearly terrified, his voice trembling.

Zhao growled and stuffed the pistol back in his belt then gunned his engine, turning around and heading back toward town, though stopping far short.

"What are we going to do?"

Zhao stared back in the direction of the roadblock then up at the jungle to their right that rose steeply from the roadside. "Go get some Molotov cocktails. We'll show these bastards that they shouldn't mess with us."

"But what about your daughter? Won't we be putting her at risk?"

Zhao grunted. "If anything happens to my daughter, then I'll kill every last one of them." He pulled out his phone and sent his daughter a text message.

Come home now!

Khwae Noi Tributary Dig Site

Kanchanaburi District, Thailand

Dara Zhao frowned at the text message from her father. Why would he want her to come home now? The school day wasn't over, and she was enjoying herself. Anything that got her out of the classroom she considered time well spent, and she found this fascinating. The jar she had helped find was incredibly cool, and the professor had let her touch it.

Smooth.

It was like glass, and his explanation for how it was done had her thinking she wanted to try it herself someday. After all, if they could do it hundreds of years ago, then surely they could do it today in town. She'd talk to her mother about it when she got home. Her mother was artistic, always creating things that would be taken to the city and sold to tourists. The world outside the village fascinated her, and she hoped one day to leave this place and see what was out there.

If her father let her.

119

He was a horrible man. He never hurt her, not physically, but words could hurt too. He was always criticizing her or her mother, shouting at them, screaming at them, terrorizing them when he drank too much. He no longer lived with them, thank goodness, but he still lived in town and far too often inserted himself into their lives.

Like now.

Was she supposed to obey him? He wanted her home right away. Which home? Hers or his? And why? She was in school, and her mother always told her that she was not to leave unless dismissed by the teacher, and then to come straight home.

Their home, not her drunken father's.

But there was one thing she had learned over the years.

Never cross Father.

She stepped back from her friends, still listening to the professor, then darted behind the tent, certain what she was doing was wrong. Yet she had no choice. Miss Panya might scold her. Her mother might yell at her.

But her father might kill her.

Royal Palace

Ayutthaya, Ayutthaya Kingdom

April 26, 1758

Uthumphon hurried toward his father's bedchambers as confusion reigned around him, guards rushing everywhere, staff in a panic. Something was going on, something serious, and the only thing he could think of was that his father had died.

His heart ached with the thought. There was no one he was closer to in this world than his father. It should be his brother, but sadly, it wasn't. He hoped in time they could set aside their differences, but Thammathibet showed no signs of maturing, and now with their father's decision to go against tradition and name him to the throne, he feared they would never be close.

He loved his brother, yet Thammathibet had brought this upon himself, and now would pay the price. His brother had never shown any interest in the throne, and a small part of him hoped that

Thammathibet would actually be happy knowing the throne wouldn't become a burden to him.

Yet he knew, despite the fact Thammathibet didn't desire the throne, he would still be hurt, and would want it because he couldn't have it. Like the child he was.

The guard opened the door and Uthumphon rushed inside to find his father appearing worse than this morning, Ferreira at his side. "Father, what is happening?"

His father said nothing, a tongue depressor in his mouth, but a voice from behind had him spinning around. "Your brother stole the Mask of Succession."

His jaw slackened at the revelation. "You can't be serious!"

"I'm afraid it is so," confirmed his father, the man's voice weak, though the anger and disappointment still evident. "When he found out you would become king and not him, he stole the mask in a rage. He is determined to become king simply to spite me." He beckoned him closer and Uthumphon stepped forward, sitting on the edge of the bed. "You must find your brother and retrieve the mask before I die. If he is wearing it when I die, then he is king."

"Where is he?"

"Find the head of my personal guard. He will know." His father took his hand. "You must find him before I die, but if you fail, and I die first, you know what to do."

Uthumphon didn't, and his eyes narrowed as he stared at his father, puzzled. "What am I to do?"

"You must kill your brother and take the mask back. Put it on, and you will be king."

Uthumphon gasped, his hand yanking away from his father. "Kill Thammathibet! I can't do that! He's my brother!"

"He may be your brother, but your duty is to the kingdom, not your family. Thousands upon thousands of lives depend upon what happens before the sun sets today. I must know that I can count on you to do the right thing, for I can feel it in my bones that I only have hours, if not minutes, left." He reached for him one more time and Uthumphon reluctantly took the hand. "Can I count on you?"

Uthumphon's shoulders slumped and his chin fell to his chest as he squeezed his eyes shut. "Yes, Father, you can count on me."

Khwae Noi Tributary Dig Site Roadblock

Kanchanaburi District, Thailand

Present Day

Zhao hurried through the trees at a crouch with three of the others, the rest idling around the bend from the roadblock, repeatedly revving their engines to provide a distraction. He held up a hand, halting the others as he spotted their targets below them, the hillside steep, their five opponents clearly concerned about his men and not the hillside.

It would be their undoing.

His intention was to send a message. If any of them died, then so be it—they shouldn't have blocked his path. They had no right to prevent him from seeing his daughter. He motioned behind him and a lighter flicked. A moment later, a lit Molotov cocktail was handed forward, and three more flared to life.

He crept forward, down the hillside, using the trees below to hold himself upright, the engines of the motorcycles still distracting those below. The canopy overhead was thick, providing them with cover, but all it would take was a single look into the jungle and he had no doubt the flames would be spotted.

He took his eyes off the target for a moment as he checked his footing, then when he looked up, he cursed as one of the white men raised his weapon, aiming it directly at them and shouting in English.

"Come out with your hands up!"

Zhao stepped out and whipped the Molotov cocktail toward the SUV, the others doing the same as he dove to the ground, an automatic weapon opening up on them. Someone screamed as he rolled back toward the trees. He gained his footing and smiled as the man who had spotted him erupted in flames. One of his fellow guards tackled him to the ground and rolled him around, battling the fire as their comrades spread out and shot into the trees.

Zhao pressed his back against a large trunk as bullets thumped into the thick wood providing him with cover, shredding the bamboo around him. The engines changed tone and he squeezed his eyes shut as the onslaught continued for a few more seconds before it suddenly stopped. He risked a peek to see his men now opening fire on the three Thais. They returned fire, mowing down half a dozen of his guys when a single Molotov cocktail sailed through the air, slamming into the far side of the SUV. It erupted in flames and his enemy fell back toward the camp, dragging their burnt comrade with them.

He stepped out from the trees and opened fire, injuring one of the Thais, but the other two quickly responded, spraying the trees with bullets as he ducked back behind his cover. One of his men cried out and he cursed at seeing him on the ground, blood pulsing from his neck. Zhao flipped around and stuck his hand out from behind the tree, emptying the trigger blindly as the enemy continued their retreat.

Then someone screamed.

A girl.

A little girl.

And his heart stopped, for he would recognize her cry from a mile away.

Khwae Noi Tributary Dig Site
Kanchanaburi District, Thailand

Acton had already taken action the moment the motorcycle engines had begun their intimidation tactic. But with the first sounds of gunfire, he realized he had been mistaken. They weren't trying to intimidate the guards at the roadblock, but divert their attention. He had ordered everyone away from the road and into the trees on the other side of the dig site, and no one had questioned him.

Achara and her assistant herded the terrified children toward the tree line as Bunthan and his people assisted. Leather and the others sprinted toward the action when a fireball erupted and someone screamed.

Acton turned to Reading. "Grenade?"

Reading shook his head. "No, I'm thinking Molotov cocktail."

More sustained gunfire was followed by another explosion.

"I think that hit the SUV," said Laura. "What should we do?"

"We need to call for help." Acton pulled out his cellphone to find they had no signal. "Satphone?"

"In the SUV," replied Laura.

Reading gave her a look. "Didn't we have a conversation about this just a couple of weeks ago?"

She rolled her eyes. "It's *with* me." She stabbed a finger at their vehicle. "It's fifty feet away."

Acton dismissed Reading's concerns. "Stay here. I'm going to get it."

A little girl screamed from down the road and the entire camp froze. He glanced over his shoulder as he sprinted toward the SUV with their belongings, and saw Achara staring at the road in horror, then spinning to do a headcount.

Yet that wasn't his concern now. If a child had been hurt, there was nothing he could do about it. He had to get their satphone so they could reach out for help. Gunfire continued to rattle down the road, far too close for comfort. He reached the SUV and yanked on the handle.

It was locked.

He turned back to the others. "Who has the key?"

Reading shook his head. "I don't know! Vidura?"

Acton rushed up the makeshift path to the road after Leather and Vidura, spotting them ahead, prone on the ground, shooting toward a bend in the road where a fire raged. "Friendly on your six!" he shouted, and Leather glanced back, gesturing for him to hold his position.

"Get back to the camp!"

"I need the keys to the SUV! It has the satphone!"

Vidura rolled to his side, fished out the keys, then hurled them toward Acton before resuming fire. Acton scurried forward and grabbed them then sprinted back toward the SUV, pressing the button on the fob, relieved to see the lights flash. He yanked open the door and grabbed their luggage, hurling them toward where Laura and the others were taking cover.

Laura scurried out and snatched one of the carry-ons, dragging it back as he rushed down the path into the camp, grabbing the other bags while they still could.

Reading shook his head at him. "You daft bastard. Stop running *toward* the gunfire!"

Acton ignored him, instead looking at Laura as she searched the bag. She yanked out the satphone triumphantly. "Who do we call?" she asked, turning it on.

"The police?" suggested Acton.

Reading shook his head. "There are no police in this area according to Vidura, and we can't trust that they even speak English."

Laura dialed a number then shoved the phone into Acton's hand. "Greg."

Acton smiled as he pressed the phone to his ear. "Good thinking."

The call was answered after a few rings by a groggy voice at the other end. "This better be good."

Gunfire punctuated the statement, and his best friend became fully alert.

"Jim, is that you?"

Milton Residence

St. Paul, Maryland

Gregory Milton, Dean of St. Paul's University and Acton's boss as well as best friend, bolted upright in bed at the sound of gunfire, for a moment forgetting he had a phone pressed to his ear. He winced in pain as his back spasmed with the abrupt movement, gripping it with his spare hand.

Gunfire could mean only one person was on the other end of the line.

"Jim, is that you?"

"Yes!"

He groaned as he reached over and turned on the nightstand lamp. "What the hell have you gotten yourself into this time?"

"The dig site is under attack, we believe by a local gang that wants to steal the artifact that was found here. There's only one road out of here and it's now blocked. I don't know how much time we've got, but you've got the details I sent you earlier, right?"

Milton nodded. "Yes, I have the location of the dig site in an email."

"Good. Get that to Dylan. See if his people can get us help. There are no police in the immediate vicinity, but he'll be able to coordinate that better than we can."

"What about your security? I thought you had a team with you?"

"They're engaging the enemy now, but we're probably outnumbered, and I doubt they have a lot of ammo. This wasn't supposed to be a gang war."

"Understood. What's your plan?"

"I don't know yet, but we can't stay here, and the only road out is blocked." There was a pause, his friend's voice replaced by the gunfire continuing in the background. "We might have to head into the trees and make our way to a city. I don't know. I have no idea where we are and what's around us."

"All right. I'll reach out to Dylan then I'll call you back."

"No, don't call us. We might be trying to hide. I'll call you when it's safe to do so."

"Understood. Be careful."

"You know me."

Milton frowned. "Yes, I do. Be. Careful."

"I will. Gotta go."

The call ended and Milton climbed out of bed as his wife, Sandra, turned on her own light. "What's going on?"

"Jim and the others are in trouble."

"Again?"

"Yes. I have to make some calls. Go back to bed."

Sandra rolled out from under the covers and grabbed a robe. "Nonsense. I'll make you some coffee. Something tells me we're going to be up for the next couple of days."

Rocky Mountain National Park, Colorado

CIA Operations Officer Dylan Kane hung by one hand from the rock outcropping. The love of his life, whose idea it was to come here today, was ten feet below, secured to the cliff face by a piton he had driven in a few minutes ago. He didn't do a lot of rock climbing, but always enjoyed the adrenaline rush, especially on a day like today where it was for fun as opposed to the job where discovery usually meant death, or at least a good beating.

Though doing it in the moonlight did reintroduce the risk of death element.

He tapped in another piton then fed the rope through as his CIA customized TAG Heuer watch signaled he had a message with a gentle pulse of electricity through his wrist. He cursed, the pattern indicating an urgent message.

"What's wrong?" asked Lee Fang from below.

"I've got an urgent message."

She groaned. "Your job is really becoming an inconvenience."

He chuckled. "I know, it's tough to be dating a superhero, isn't it?"

She eyed him. "Let's not get carried away."

He laughed and peered down. "Do you think we're high enough?"

She checked. "Yeah, I think so."

"You *think*?"

She grinned up at him. "Only one way to find out!" She disconnected from the rope and leaned away from the rock, executing a perfect rearward-facing dive before spreading her arms and legs out into an arch, her parachute ripping out a moment later. He unclipped and pushed away, twisting his body to reorient himself, then shoved his chest out as his limbs extended, spreadeagle. He pulled his cord and his chute yanked out, jerking at him and killing his speed, turning his hurtling plunge into a more manageable, and survivable, rate.

He checked for four good corners as he grabbed his toggles, guiding himself away from the mountain they had been climbing and toward their parked car below. A few minutes later, they were gathering their chutes as several other crazies about to begin their own moonlight climb applauded. He smiled and waved, pleasantries exchanged, then stripped out of his gear as Fang did the same.

She jerked her chin toward his watch. "Next time I plan something, leave that behind."

He closed the rear hatch. "You know the deal. You date me, you date the watch." He tossed her the keys. "You drive. I have to log in."

He climbed into the passenger seat and unlocked the glove compartment with a tap of his watch, retrieving his cellphone. He logged in as Fang guided them toward home, and he cursed when he saw who the message was from. He brought up the voicemail from Milton, putting it on speaker.

"Hi, Dylan, Gregory Milton here. I just got an urgent call from Jim. They're at a dig site in Thailand and a local gang has just attacked them. They are trapped and need help. Apparently, there are no police in the vicinity, and they don't know what to do. They're going to try and escape through the jungle, but don't know where to go. They need help. Is there any way your people can contact the local authorities, or get in there to help them? You have my number. I'll be awaiting your call."

Kane pursed his lips as he forwarded the voicemail to his best friend, Chris Leroux. Acton was Kane's former archaeology professor, and had helped him decide what he wanted to do with his life. That decision had him dropping out of college and joining the Army, where he excelled, eventually recruited into the CIA. The man could have just as easily counseled him into staying in school, but he hadn't. He had instead encouraged him to follow his heart, and his heart had him fighting terrorism, not reading books. Acton and his now-wife, Laura, were a pain in his ass sometimes, but they also proved helpful far too many times to count. He would do anything he could for them, as they would for him.

They were family.

And family dropped everything when the call came.

Fang glanced over at him as she guided them down the winding road. "Are you heading to Thailand?"

He shook his head. "No. This will be over long before I can get there. Hopefully we've got someone in the area that can reach them in time."

Operations Center 2, CIA Headquarters

Langley, Virginia

CIA Analyst Supervisor Chris Leroux, nearing the end of a nightshift, read the priority message from Kane, then listened to the voicemail from Milton. And cursed. Yet again, the professors were in trouble, though he supposed they could hardly be blamed for being attacked by a local gang. Then again, they were the type that might have provoked it.

His second-in-command, Sonya Tong, turned in her chair, regarding him. "You've got that look."

He glanced at her as he fit his headset in place. "Oh? What look is that?"

"That annoyed look, like you're about to deal with something you shouldn't need to be dealing with."

He chuckled. "You know me *way* too well." He gestured at his monitor. "It looks like the professors are in trouble again."

A round of mock groans erupted from the room.

He wagged a hand at them over his shoulder. "Let's give them the benefit of the doubt until I find out what's going on." He forwarded the message to Tong. "I just sent you the message. Start pulling up anything you can based on what you hear. You'll be focusing on Thailand."

"I'm on it."

Leroux pressed the earpiece a little tighter as Milton answered. "Hello?"

"Hello, Mr. Milton. This is Chris Leroux. I understand there is a situation involving Professor Acton?"

"Oh, hi, Chris, thanks for getting back to me so quickly. Yes, apparently they're being attacked by—"

"Yes, I listened to your voicemail. I'm going to need their exact position if you have it."

"I have some GPS coordinates that he emailed me after his plans changed." Milton rhymed off the numbers and Leroux jotted them down before handing them to Tong.

"Who's with him?"

"Laura, Tommy Granger, Mai Trinh, and Hugh Reading. Plus their security detail."

"Leather?"

"Yes."

"How big a team?"

"I have no idea, sorry."

"All right, here's what I want you to do. I'm going to give you an email address then you're going to send me everything you know.

Names, why they were there, who they met with, hotels, travel arrangements, absolutely anything you can think of no matter how insignificant it might seem. Send me whatever you've got in the next ten minutes, then send me more if you have it, every ten minutes. I don't want any delays while you try to put everything in one email. Understood?"

"Yes."

Leroux gave him the email address then ended the call. He turned to Tong. "Do we have anything?"

She nodded toward the massive displays wrapping around the front of the room, a satellite image appearing. He cursed. It showed a dried-up riverbed stretching from east to west with a road on the north side, and what appeared to be an archaeological dig site on the south. A fire was raging on the road to the northeast, and muzzles flashed nearby.

Then he spotted something that sent a chill through his spine as he rose, stepping closer to the display. He pointed. "Is that a school bus?"

Tong gasped as she worked her station, isolating the vehicle and opening another window to the right of the main image. There was no doubt. It was a school bus.

He turned to the others. "Start isolating targets. We need to know if there are children there, and if we can identify our people. I need to know who the friendlies are, and who the hostiles are. Let's treat this like we just found one of our teams and they're in deep shit." He headed for the door. "Sonya, reach out to the Thais. Let them know what's happening. I'm going to talk to the Chief and let him know what's going on, and see if he can liaise with them. This could turn into a horror story if we don't act quickly."

Khwae Noi Tributary Dig Site Roadblock
Kanchanaburi District, Thailand

Zhao erupted from the trees with a roar, firing blindly at the retreating guards as he rushed toward where he had heard his daughter scream. He reached the other side of the road and dove, sliding over the edge and partway down the muddy embankment. He spotted a flash of bright green near the former riverbed and continued to scramble toward it as tears welled.

For there was no doubt it was his daughter's favorite dress that he had spotted, worn only on special occasions, the school trip where she was to be shown what she had discovered apparently worthy in her and her mother's eyes.

He skidded to a halt, his feet slipping in the mud, and fell beside her. His gasp hurt his chest as he spotted the blood soaking her stomach, her tiny chest heaving, her face wincing with every move. Dara's cheeks were stained with tears as she whimpered, then she cried out as she recognized her father.

141

"Father! They hurt me!"

He grabbed her and held her tight, sobbing with the realization it hadn't been them at all, it had been him, firing blindly. "What were you doing there? You should have been at the dig!"

"You said to come home!" she protested, her tone suggesting she was terrified of getting in trouble for doing something wrong. This was his fault. He had told her to go home, he had blindly fired the bullet.

He had killed his own daughter.

He brushed the hair from her face and stared into her eyes so much like her mother's. "I'm sorry."

She peered down at her stomach and the blood saturating her dress. "Tell Mother I'm sorry I ruined my dress."

He clenched his fists, focusing on the pain of his nails digging into his palms, fighting back the tears. "I'm sure she can clean it. You know how good she is at such things."

"I'm cold. I want to go home."

He scooped her up and carried her up the hill, the gunfire from both sides coming to a halt as he stepped onto the road. A horrifying sigh escaped her lungs and he rested her on the ground, holding her face as he smiled at her while she faded away. He checked for a pulse but found nothing.

She was gone.

He twisted his head skyward and roared in anguish at what he had done, what they had done. While he might have fired the shot that killed her, it was the others that had created the situation. He picked her up and held her tight, turning toward his enemy as they slowly

142

retreated, their weapons at the ready, the horror on their faces lost on him.

"You tell whoever you work for that I'm coming for them! They killed my daughter. And now every single one of you is going to die!"

"Listen, we can talk about—"

He glared at the man. "There is nothing to discuss. Before this day is out, the Red Wa will kill you all."

"We have children here. At least let them go."

He shook his head as he held his limp daughter tighter. "By tonight, the entire village will suffer as I do now." He walked toward his men. "Tonight, everyone dies!"

Khwae Noi Tributary Dig Site
Kanchanaburi District, Thailand

Acton rose along with the others as the gunfire stopped. Leather was on his feet, beckoning the others to hurry, and his heart sank as he saw two bodies dragged by the group that had set up the roadblock.

He turned to Tommy and Mai. "Check the vehicles for med kits."

They both headed for the two remaining SUVs as Leather joined them, helping carry one of his men, moaning in agony. Acton resisted the urge to cringe as he caught a look at the man, suffering from second and third-degree burns on his face, the rest of his uniform scorched.

"What the bloody hell happened to him?" asked Reading as he took a knee and began gently removing the man's equipment, his first aid training as a police officer taking over.

"Molotov cocktail," replied one of the Thai guards. "They hit him then hit our vehicle. The road is blocked for the moment, but that's the least of our worries."

Tommy returned with a med kit and Laura joined Reading as they treated the wounded man. "I thought I heard a girl scream. Is there someone else that was hurt?"

Bunthan rushed over with Achara. "One of the children is missing," said Bunthan, breathlessly.

Achara was in a state of near panic. "Dara is missing! We can't find her!"

Laura looked up at her. "Wait, wasn't she the daughter of that gang leader?"

"Yes."

One of Leather's locals cursed. "That explains it, then. The guy who seemed to be behind this shot a little girl. He was firing blindly. I didn't see her hiding by the road until she screamed. She fell over the side to the riverbed and he went after her. He brought her out a few minutes later. She was dead."

Acton exchanged a look with Reading. "That can't be good."

The local shook his head. "No. He said he's going to kill everyone here, including the children."

"Can he?" asked Reading. "I mean, did it look like they had the firepower to take us on?"

"He might not have, but he said, 'Before this day is out, the Red Wa will kill you all.'"

"Who are the Red Wa?" asked Mai, her voice trembling.

"The biggest organized crime gang in Thailand."

Acton turned to Achara. "Is this true? Is he a member?"

She shook her head. "No. I mean, not really. He likes to pretend he is, and I think they might have some sort of agreement, but I don't know. Nobody ever took him very seriously."

Leather frowned. "Well, he's acting pretty serious now. He could be returning in numbers, and we have limited ammo."

Acton pulled at his hair as he stared at the tree line, children's faces emerging from the jungle. "We can't stay here."

"No, we can't."

"But where do we go? We can't just run into the jungle and hide. They'll hunt us down or we'll get lost and die in there."

Leather turned to Vidura. "What's the nearest town?"

Vidura pulled out his phone but Achara answered for him. "We need to get to Kanchanaburi. It's southeast of here, about fifty kilometers. It's big and will have police that can protect us."

Laura glanced up over her shoulder at the children. "That's pretty far to take children and two wounded men."

"One wounded man," said one of the locals. "Our man didn't make it."

Reading rose, indicating Leather's man. "And he's not going to make it if we don't get him to a hospital. His burns are bad. I don't know what to do with him, and that med kit is pretty limited."

Acton regarded the wounded man, here because of him. "We can't just leave him here. The gang won't just kill him, they'll torture him."

Leather's injured man reached up and grabbed his boss by the leg. "Leave me. Just give me a weapon. I'll only slow you down."

"Bollocks," echoed all the Brits in the group.

Acton turned to Bunthan. "Do you have a stretcher?"

Bunthan nodded and disappeared into a nearby tent as Acton crunched the numbers. "If we have to cover fifty kilometers, that's thirty miles. With the kids and this terrain, the best we could probably hope for is maybe two miles an hour. We're going to have to take breaks as well, maybe stop overnight, so the best we're looking at is perhaps twenty miles in a day, and that's assuming nothing goes wrong. We're looking at slogging it through the jungle until at least the end of day tomorrow."

Leather agreed. "I don't see that we have a choice. We'll be out of ammo within minutes if we get in a sustained fight with significant numbers, and once we're out, we're dead."

"Then let's plan this right," said Laura as Bunthan returned with the stretcher. She stepped aside as two of Leather's men helped their comrade onto it. "I suggest we get a bearing, and Chayan and Achara, you take the children and the wounded into the trees now, and cover as much distance as you can. The rest of us will gather all the supplies we can carry. Food, water, medical, lights. Everything to survive for two days."

Acton clapped his hands together. "Sounds like a plan. And let's hit that kitchen. There could be some good weapons in there. And we can use the knives to fashion our own weapons. I have a feeling before we get out of this, it could devolve pretty rapidly."

Leather started barking orders to his men as Bunthan gathered his people around to explain what was going on. Within minutes, their wounded man had been carried into the jungle with the children following, and everyone else was collecting supplies.

And in the distance, a motorcycle engine reminded them they were on a tight deadline.

Director Morrison's Office, CIA Headquarters

Langley, Virginia

Leroux rushed into Leif Morrison's office, the National Clandestine Service Chief for the CIA peering intently at his laptop. Morrison pointed at a vacant chair in front of his desk, saying nothing as he continued to read. He finished a moment later then turned his attention to his guest.

"I assume you're here about this email I just got from Kane."

Leroux's eyebrows rose slightly. "Oh? I wasn't aware he contacted you too. If it's about the situation in Thailand, then yes."

Morrison sighed. "These professors are going to drive me into an early retirement."

"In fairness, sir, I got the impression they weren't looking for us to intervene, but simply to contact the proper authorities before it was too late."

"And have we?"

"Sonya is on it, but…"

Morrison tossed his glasses on his desk. "But what?"

"Well, it looks like children are involved, and our people—"

"Our?"

Leroux shrugged. "It's kind of hard not to think of them as our people. They've been involved so much—"

"Too much."

"Yes, sir, *too* much, with us over the years, it's hard not to think of them as part of the family. And in this case, it doesn't look like they ran toward the danger." Leroux held up his phone. "While I was waiting to see you, Greg Milton sent me an email with the details as he knows them."

Morrison leaned back. "All right, why were they there?"

"They arranged a reunion with Mai Trinh's father at the Vietnam-Cambodia border."

Morrison's eyebrows shot up. "Seriously? How the hell did they manage that? He's been blacklisted, hasn't he?"

"Last I heard, yes, sir. But they managed it somehow. Before they left, they received a message from the son of a friend, who's an archaeologist in Thailand, that he had found an artifact he wanted them to see, so they tacked that on to the end of their trip."

"So, if Mai is there, I assume her boyfriend as well?"

"Yes, sir, Tommy Granger. He's been helpful—"

"Yeah, yeah, I know. And Agent Reading is with them too, according to Kane. He's been…" Morrison pursed his lips. "We have assets in Thailand that might be able to help, but Kane has a better idea."

"Oh?"

"He already reached out to Bravo Team."

Leroux leaned forward eagerly. "Please tell me they're available."

"They're not. And besides, we couldn't send them in officially regardless. However, they just wrapped up a training mission in South Korea. Three of them stayed behind for a few days while the rest headed off on another job. Apparently, one of them has family there."

"That would be Niner."

"Well, Kane is reaching out to see if they want to alter their vacation plans. If they agree, we'll need to arrange false identities, the works, to get them in, then supply them when they arrive."

Leroux rose. "I'll get on it right away, sir."

"You're assuming they're going to say yes."

"Sir, I know these men. There's no way in hell they're going to say no."

Sung Household

Suwon-si, Republic of Korea

Sergeant Carl "Niner" Sung leaned back in his chair and groaned in ecstasy as he slowly chewed his grandmother's barbecue. His head lolled to the side at his best friend sitting beside him, Sergeant Leon "Atlas" James. "Didn't I tell you she's the best cook in the world?"

Atlas continued to attack the meal, his plate continually topped up by Niner's female relatives, none of them letting him, Atlas, or Sergeant Gerry "Jimmy Olsen" Hudson go hungry. The meal had been ongoing for at least two hours, and Niner swore he had the meat sweats, but he was afraid to stop.

It might insult the cadre of cooks.

One thing he had learned the last time he visited here was that the meal didn't stop until the food ran out. The problem was he wasn't accustomed to eating like this. Sure, he would attack a pizza on occasion, but as part of 1st Special Forces Operational Detachment—Delta, or as the common person on the street called it, the Delta Force, he had to be in peak shape all the time. Eating like this was not something he did.

Yet his muscled friend Atlas was just treating it like he was carbo-loading for an extended session with the weights. Jimmy, appearing equally stuffed, glanced at their large friend then reached over and squeezed a massive bicep.

"Are these muscles or extra stomachs?"

"Can't talk, eating," replied Atlas as he took another mouthful, the empty space on his plate immediately filled by an alert cousin. He paused then gave both of them a stern look. "If either of you mentions any of this to Vanessa, they won't find the bodies."

Niner grunted. "Sure they will. They'll just have to pump your stomach."

Atlas rolled his eyes, tossing his head back. "Sooo good. I'm leaving here with recipes. I have to have Vanessa make this for me."

"I doubt they'll give them up. Family secrets."

"Ask."

"They won't—"

"If you want to live to see the morning, you ask and you ask now."

Niner grinned at Jimmy as Atlas leaned forward, continuing the impressive show. Niner turned to his grandmother, switching to Korean. "My friend wants the recipes for all this. His girlfriend is a chef, and he wants her to cook this for him when he gets back home."

She firmly shook her head. "No. Family only."

Niner put an arm over Atlas' shoulders and Jimmy looked at him, concerned. "Niner, buddy, your hand is getting a little close to his mouth. Careful."

Niner moved his hand but didn't remove his arm. "But, Grandma, he *is* family. This man has saved my life more times than I can count. If it weren't for him, I wouldn't be here today."

His grandmother pursed her lips, regarding the eating-machine, then threw her hands up in the air. "All right! All right! He's family, he gets the recipes."

Niner smiled and leaned over, giving her a kiss on the cheek. "Thank you, Grandma!" He turned to Atlas, switching back to English. "You're part of the family now. She's giving you the recipes."

Atlas flashed her a smile and a thumbs-up.

"Only one problem, though."

Atlas eyed his friend. "What's that?"

"You'll have to break up with Vanessa."

The feeding frenzy halted. "Huh? Why?"

"Well, now that you're family, you'll have to bring home a nice Korean girl the next time you're visiting."

Atlas eyed his plate and Jimmy agreed with Niner. "Yeah, he's not joking. They're pretty serious about this kind of stuff."

Atlas gave Jimmy a look then Niner. "I'll deal with you two later." He shoved his chopsticks back into his pile of food. "I've got work to do."

Niner roared with laughter and pulled his vibrating phone out of his pocket. He swiped his thumb across the screen and pressed it to his ear, not recognizing the number. "Hello?"

"Hey, buddy, it's Dylan."

Niner's eyebrows shot up and he rose, excusing himself. Kane had served in the Unit before joining the CIA, and while they were friends, he never called. Never. "Dylan? Did you just spot the third horseman of the apocalypse and are calling to find out if I've seen the fourth?"

"Huh?"

"You never call me, dude!"

"While I'd love to say it's a social call, I don't like you that much, so you'd know it was bullshit."

"I'm hurt. I'm really hurt," deadpanned Niner.

Kane laughed. "Listen, we've got a situation developing in Thailand. The professors—"

"Of course."

"—are at a dig site in a remote area with a bunch of schoolchildren, and are being attacked by a local gang. Apparently, they want something they have. I'm waiting to get more details. Anyway, I need some muscle there, and a little birdie told me that you, Atlas, and Jimmy are in Korea. If you leave now, you can be in position by morning."

Niner glanced back into the room where the festivities were. He loved being here, but he owed the professors. They all did. And just the mention that children were involved pretty much settled it. "I assume this is all off the books?"

155

"Completely, though Langley is going to help with logistics and intel. If you're in, I'll have them send you your travel itinerary and then arrange for someone to meet, brief, and equip you when you land. Are you in?"

"I'm in, and I'm sure Jimmy is. Atlas might have to be hauled from the food kicking and screaming, but he'll be in. Send me the deets."

"Will do. Thanks. I wish I could be there but I'm just too far away to get there in time to do any good."

"Don't worry about it. You'd just get in the way." Niner ended the call before Kane could defend himself, then stepped back into the room, delivering the bad news in Korean. "I'm sorry, folks, but we're going to have to leave. There's an emergency and they need us."

Groans filled the room and Atlas stopped eating. "What's going on?"

"That was Dylan. The Doc and Laura are in trouble in Thailand. A bunch of schoolchildren are involved. We need to get there ASAP."

Atlas wiped his mouth and rose, patting his slightly bulging stomach. "Thank you, ladies, that was deeelish." He turned to Niner. "You *will* be getting me those recipes. Don't you think I forgot just because we're leaving early."

"I wouldn't dream of it. Now let's go."

Atlas grabbed the back of his chair. "Umm, I think I better make a pitstop before we hit the road."

Niner groaned. "Dude! Try to take it easy on their plumbing. Things over here aren't exactly designed for colons like yours."

Khwae Noi Tributary Dig Site
Kanchanaburi District, Thailand

Bunthan checked over both shoulders before ducking into his tent. He headed directly for the far corner and pulled up the tarp then scooped away the dirt covering the box holding the jade mask. He opened it then gently removed the relic. He wrapped it in a nearby towel then stuffed it into his backpack. He returned the box to the hole then shoveled the dirt over it with his hand before flipping the tarp into place. He slung his pack over his shoulders then headed outside to rejoin the flurry of activity.

Achara and Photsi had left with the children and the wounded soldier, and his students had already grabbed all the food and water they could fit into their backpacks, each of them now gripping a knife from the kitchen, or a makeshift weapon like a pipe or hammer.

It was terrifying.

And it was all his fault. He should have fought for a bigger budget so they could have had security here the entire time. Yet as he looked at

157

what was going on, eight heavily armed men wasn't enough, and he at best might have scrounged the funding for two. He sighed. He never should have let the children search the dig site, but then who would have thought they'd stumble upon something so valuable? And who would have thought that the girl who found it would be the daughter of the local crime lord?

He growled to himself as Sanun rushed up. "I think we've got everything we're going to need. We should get moving."

Bunthan agreed then pointed toward the trees. "Gather the others and get going. I want to catch up to the children as quickly as possible." Sanun nodded then called to the others, leading them toward the jungle. Bunthan joined Acton and his people. "We've got everything we can carry."

Acton slung his own backpack over his shoulders, then expertly checked the weapon that had belonged to the dead Thai guard. "Then let's get the hell out of here." He jerked his chin toward the road and the increasing sounds of revving motorcycle engines. "Something tells me they're not going to be much longer."

Leather took charge. "All right, let's move!"

Acton led the way with Laura, Reading, Tommy, and Mai on his heels, the security team taking up the rear. Within minutes, they were in the jungle and out of sight of the camp, following the far too loud group ahead of them. They needed to put some serious distance between themselves and the dig site before Red Wa arrived, otherwise they'd track them down with little trouble.

And slaughter them all.

A thought occurred to him and he cursed.

"What?" asked Laura.

"In all the excitement, I forgot all about the mask that Achara told us about. We should have just left it out there for them to find. That might have been enough to have them leave us alone."

Laura pushed aside a tree branch. "Do you think Chayan forgot?"

"He must have. He didn't say anything to me, but then again, we barely said anything to each other since we got here. Too much has been going on."

"You're right. If Achara hadn't told us about the mask, we wouldn't even know about it."

Acton sighed. "He must have forgotten about it." He shook his head, knowing what he would have done if the roles were reversed. "No, he didn't forget it."

Laura agreed. "You wouldn't have and neither would I."

"And we'd be stupid enough to take it with us."

She smiled at him. "Well, you would be."

He chuckled. "When we catch up to him, we'll have to ask. It's too late to leave it behind now, but we might be able to use it as a bargaining chip later."

"Is it too late? We could catch up to him, get it, then run it back."

Acton was about to agree when the motorcycle engines roared louder.

Red Wa was on the move.

Muban Chong Sadao

Kanchanaburi District, Thailand

Zhao carried his daughter's body into her mother's home, his tears dried up, his guilt gone. In the short ride here, accompanied by two of his men, he had absolved himself of all responsibility. It was those at the dig that were responsible. The professor had lied, supported by his people. Achara had obviously been in on it, which meant her assistant, Miss Photsi, was involved.

And the armed guards that had arrived conveniently only days after his daughter had discovered whatever it was the academics were hiding? They were only there for one reason. To keep him from what was rightfully his family's.

They all had to die.

But it wasn't just them. The town had embraced these outsiders, had welcomed the city folk into their homes and businesses, happily took their money and socialized with them. And now, for making them welcome, they would pay too. Their children would die, just like his daughter.

Everyone would suffer from what had happened here.

Dara's mother glared at him. He was not welcome here at any time. "What do you think you're doing? She's still sup—" Her jaw dropped when she saw the bloodstained dress, the bullet having traveled through her tiny body. She screamed, a horrifying outburst that curdled his blood. She rushed forward, taking Dara's face in her hands, gently slapping her cheeks in a useless attempt to wake her up.

"She's dead." He placed Dara on the couch as her grandparents rushed into the room, along with several visiting relatives who had been in the backyard.

"What happened?" asked Dara's grandfather as the women rushed to the couch, surrounding the body.

"She was shot," he murmured.

"By whom?"

The truth would do no one any good, and besides, even if the bullet did originate from his gun, it was only fired because the guards were firing at him. She was dead because of them. "The guards at the dig site."

"Guards? What guards?" asked Dara's mother.

"They arrived this morning, I guess. I went to see Dara, to see what she had found, but they wouldn't let us pass then they shot at us. She was killed by accident." The lie had his stomach churning, bile flowing, and he stumbled out the front door, emptying his stomach on the lawn. He bent over, grabbing his knees as he continued to wretch. A hand patting his back had him snap back to reality, forcing the clouds of guilt, threatening to force him to reveal the truth, scurrying back into the recesses of his mind.

He stood upright then stared back through the door, the woman he had once loved, before he had lost his way, still wailing along with her relatives. He faced what should have been his father-in-law, but couldn't look him in the eye. "Tell her I'm sorry." He turned but was stopped by a hand on his arm.

"Where are you going?"

"To get revenge."

"No, let's call the police. These people need to be punished for what they've done."

Zhao shook his head. "No, there's no justice for people like us. City folk always get away with everything." He stepped over to his bike and straddled it. "I'll deliver the justice Dara deserves. I swear it." He fired up the engine then turned back to the road, gunning the motor.

"Don't do anything stupid! Things are bad enough!"

But Zhao ignored the warning. Today, he would kill everyone responsible, take what belonged to his daughter, and earn his bones.

When Red Wa heard about what he was about to do, there would never be any doubt he was worthy of joining their ranks, and he could leave this miserable village once and for all.

For there was nothing left here for him.

En Route to Kanchanaburi

Kanchanaburi District, Thailand

Acton cursed as yet again the call he was placing to Milton dropped. He glanced up at the thick canopy of trees overhead and shook his head. The one thing they had that might make a difference, the satphone, was useless.

"No luck?" asked Laura as she glanced over her shoulder, following Reading, Tommy, and Mai.

"Nada. The trees are too thick, I guess. We're going to have to wait to find an opening."

Tommy slowed up slightly. "Are you getting any kind of signal?"

"It's dropping in and out. It never stays connected long enough to complete the call."

"Then don't bother. You'll just waste the battery. Send a text message instead. It only needs a brief connection to send."

Acton groaned. "I keep forgetting that." His thumbs furiously attacked the antiquated keypad and he sent a simple message to Milton.

Heading SE to Kanchanaburi. ETA late tomorrow.

He hit send then smiled triumphantly as the message was successfully sent. "I'll turn it off in five minutes, just in case Greg wants to send a response."

"Don't bother. Just turn it on in five minutes, and if he sent something, it will come through then. No point wasting juice."

"Smart thinking. I knew we brought you along for some reason."

Tommy grinned. "I'm not just another pretty face."

Reading cursed ahead of them as a branch snapped back and smacked him in the face.

"Sorry," said Mai meekly, then her eyes bulged as she caught a glimpse of his face. "You're bleeding!"

Reading wiped the back of his hand against his cheek and it came away bloody. "It's not your fault. We're following each other too closely."

Laura caught up to him. "Let me take a look at that." She was the only one he would let examine him. She lifted his mosquito netting and peered at the wound in the dim light before patting his cheek. "It's not near your eye, and it looks clean. We can stop and bandage it—"

Reading shook his head. "No. We need to keep moving as fast as we can. We don't have time for scratches." He turned back to Acton. "We're moving too slowly."

Acton regarded his friend, soaked in sweat, his chest already heaving. "Slow and steady. We can't risk anyone getting injured, and we can't leave anyone behind. We'll be caught up to the others soon enough."

"Let's hope not, otherwise the group is *really* going slow."

Acton handed his friend a water bottle. "Drink. You're going to dehydrate."

Reading was about to protest, probably something about not drinking another man's water, but one look from Laura had him taking several healthy gulps before handing the bottle back. "Thanks."

"Keep it. We've got plenty."

Reading grunted. "You won't be saying that tomorrow."

"Let's worry about tomorrow, tomorrow. We just need to cover as much distance as we can. If we're lucky, they might lose interest. If we're really lucky, they might never take any interest."

A burst of gunfire erupted behind them, too close for comfort, and Leather indicated for them to keep moving as his team came to a halt. Laura squeezed Acton's hand and he returned the gesture before they kept moving forward. They were definitely going too slow, and unfortunately, there was nothing they could do about the cause.

Reading was in pain.

Operations Center 2, CIA Headquarters
Langley, Virginia

Leroux ended the call with Milton, the dean passing on the text message he had just received from Acton and reviewing the email he had sent with all the details he could remember. He turned to the team's wunderkind, Randy Child. "I've sent you the professor's satphone info. Keep an eye on it. They'll probably be preserving the battery, so don't be surprised if you don't get a signal, but I want to be notified whenever we can send them info."

Child spun in his chair. "You'll know the second I do."

Leroux turned to Tong. "They're heading southeast toward a place called Kanchanaburi. They think they might arrive by tomorrow evening."

Marc Therrien, one of his senior analysts, whistled from the back of the room. "That's a long hike, especially with kids. How the hell do they think they're going to be able to keep ahead of the group that's after them?"

Child faced the much older man. "What are they supposed to do? It's not like they have a choice."

Therrien regarded him. "I realize that. But the professors rarely do anything without a plan."

Leroux responded rather than letting an unintentional spat develop. "I'm not sure there was much time for a plan. From what we saw in that satellite footage, they've got about a dozen children with them, one man on a stretcher, plus civilians of various ages and physical ability. We have to assume that the hostiles are younger, fit, and motivated for whatever reason."

"But over twenty-four hours?"

"That's without help. We need to get help to them so we can cut that time way down." Leroux faced Tong. "I sent you that email from Milton. It's got the name of his friend in Thailand whose son is in charge of the expedition. Apparently, he's a wealthy businessman. Let's try to track him down. He might be able to use his connections to get help into the area."

"I'm on it. So far, we haven't been able to reach anybody in the area. I've got the embassy on it, but they're not optimistic. Apparently, there's only one gang that operates in that area, and the locals won't be too crazy about getting involved without some serious help. And even if they can get some help in from Bangkok, it's going to take time to reach them, if they can even find them in that jungle."

Leroux exhaled loudly, his lips vibrating. "It's never easy, is it? Let's try and reach his father. Someone with money agitating on that end might just get the action we need."

Khwae Noi Tributary Dig Site
Kanchanaburi District, Thailand

Zhao pulled to a halt at the dig site, pleased to see several dozen men looting the camp. Clearly the calls he had ordered had been heeded, and they had more than enough to deal with these city folk. He hailed Chula, and his friend rushed over, concern on his face.

"Are you all right?"

Zhao shrugged. "I will be once we've killed those bastards."

"How did her mother take it?"

"How do you think?"

"Does she blame you?"

Zhao glared at him. "Why would she?"

Chula stepped back. "Sorry, I just meant she blames you for everything, so…"

Zhao shook his head. "We know who's to blame here." He stabbed a finger at the camp. "It's these liars and thieves." He surveyed the area. "Any sign of them?"

"No. We found one body, though."

"The guy I shot or the burnt one?"

"Shot. No sign of the burnt one."

"That means they're carrying him. That will slow them down." Zhao glanced at the abandoned vehicles. "Check if they're working. We should be able to sell them in the city."

Chula turned and whistled at one of their men, pointing at the SUVs. "See if you can get those running."

"Yes, sir!"

"Have you found anything yet?" asked Zhao.

"It looks like they left in a hurry. They left computers and all kinds of equipment here."

"We'll sell it, but that's not what I'm talking about."

Chula frowned. "Nothing made from jade, no. Just a bunch of jars and crap."

"And the one they tried to trick us with?"

Chula pointed at a table near a large tent, the jar in question sitting on it. "I'm guessing that's it. I checked it out. It's worthless, just like you said."

"Any sign of where they went?"

"Footprints lead into the trees. I've sent a few guys in to track them. They can't have gotten far."

"Good. Leave a few guys behind to gather up anything of value and direct any new arrivals." Zhao headed for the trees. "Everyone else with me. We've got bones to earn."

"Sir!"

He spun toward one of his men beckoning him from a large tent. "What?"

"You've got to see this!"

He headed for the tent and stepped inside to find two of his men standing over a hole dug in the ground near the rear corner, a tarp flipped aside. "What's this?"

One of the men pointed. "We found this box buried here."

Zhao bent over and picked up the metal box, his heart pounding with excitement. This could be what they were searching for. It was in the main tent, which he was sure the professor used as his office, it was in a hole hidden under the floor, and it had a lock on it. It was obviously used for storing valuables.

He frowned as he found the lid unlocked. He flipped it open and cursed. It was empty. He threw it on the floor and stormed from the tent, heading for the trees. There was no doubt in his mind now. Dara had found something extremely valuable, and the city folk had taken it with them.

En Route to Kanchanaburi

Kanchanaburi District, Thailand

Bunthan pushed through the trees, his students and staff spread out behind him. The children should be just ahead, and while they were of course a concern, he was more desperate to find Achara. Once with her, he would rest a little easier, for the light was fading in the already dim jungle, and he feared they might not find each other.

"Look!"

He spun to see Sanun pointing ahead, just to their right. He peered into the trees and spotted movement. "Achara!" he hissed.

"Chayan? Is that you?"

"Yes." He made a beeline for the voice and rushed into Achara's arms, hugging her hard. "Oh, thank goodness!"

She leaned her forehead against his chest. "I was afraid we'd lost you."

"So was I." He turned to his team. "Everyone pair up with a child. Carry them if you have to, but we need to keep moving as fast as we can."

His people did as asked, and within moments they were continuing forward, his hand gripping Achara's. He heard something ahead and spotted more movement. A voice challenged them.

"Identify yourselves."

"It's Professor Bunthan and my team, as well as the children."

"Follow my voice, Professor."

They did and he exchanged handshakes with those carrying the wounded soldier. "I'm glad we caught up to you. I was beginning to think we'd stay separated in the dark."

One of the Thai guards shook his hand. "I'm Kasem, Professor. I need two volunteers to carry the stretcher. We need a rest."

Sanun stepped forward. "I'll help."

Another of Bunthan's students raised a hand. "I will too."

Kasem slapped them both on the back. "Excellent. Then let's get going. There's no time to waste. Soon it will be too dark to keep moving."

His students picked up the stretcher and Kasem led the way, checking a compass before adjusting their bearing. Bunthan followed in silence, his mind racing with what Kasem had just said. Surely, when it got dark, they wouldn't be stopping, would they? Zhao and his insane posse wouldn't, he was certain.

Achara yanked on his arm and he turned. "We can't stop!" she hissed. "It'd be suicide!"

He had to agree. "I know. I don't know what he's talking about." He leaned even closer to her as they continued forward. "He's not in charge. I'm sure he'll be overruled."

Then Achara asked the all-important question. "Who *is* in charge?"

And for the first time since this had begun, he realized he didn't know. Acton had certainly been issuing orders and everyone was following them, and he had happily conceded control to the older man, but this was *his* expedition. He was responsible for the students and staff, and the children and their guardians were his guests. Even Acton and the others were there at his request as guests.

There was no doubt who was in charge. It was him, yet simply acknowledging that fact had his pulse pounding in his ears. He didn't want the responsibility. He wasn't prepared for it. He had no idea what to do in a situation like this.

All he did know was that there was no way they could stop, darkness or not.

Rear Guard, En Route to Kanchanaburi
Kanchanaburi District, Thailand

Leather raised a fist, bringing his team to a halt. They were deliberately not catching up to the others as he wanted a buffer between the civilians and themselves, though he also didn't want to fall too far behind in case some of the enemy made it past them.

Like the three that were barreling toward them in blind pursuit.

It was obviously an advance party sent to find them, otherwise there'd be a lot more noise. He understood why they had been sent, but it didn't mean you didn't keep quiet when in pursuit of your target.

It would be their undoing.

Using hand signals, he spread his men out, the two on their flanks readying their rifles as he and the others drew knives. He wanted this silent and quick. If they could eliminate these three then hide the bodies, it could buy them time, and they needed every minute. Night was coming, and it would delay them, perhaps even bring them to a complete halt. Their enemy had the luxury of not worrying about revealing themselves once they had numbers. His people did not. They had to travel in the dark—torches or flashlights would reveal their position in the pitch black.

What they would do, he wasn't certain yet, but he was already developing a plan that involved delaying tactics and making the enemy think twice about traveling in the dark. But before he could finalize anything, he had to take care of business.

He pressed against a large tree trunk, his blade ready, the sound of branches snapping and men cursing approaching rapidly. His trained ear told him that his target was coming from the right, and he readied himself. The man rushed past and Leather reached out, grabbing him from behind and plunging his blade into the man's kidneys as he covered his victim's mouth, muffling his cry. He twisted the blade then yanked it free and finished him off by slicing his throat.

He checked left and right to see the other two targets down, all three eliminated silently. He lowered his man to the ground then searched him, stripping him of weapons and ammo as the others did the same. Every gun, every bullet, that they could introduce into the battle on their side could mean the difference between life and death, and he intended to survive this.

He dragged the corpse into the hollow of a large tree and covered it with leaves, then did a cursory check to make sure the others had done the same before continuing after the civilians.

And finalizing his plan.

Red Wa Position, En Route to Kanchanaburi

Kanchanaburi District, Thailand

Zhao pressed forward, searching for the telltale signs indicating the path his prey had taken, and wasn't disappointed. By his count, there had to be thirty people making their way through the jungle ahead of them, including men, women, and children, and they had left a distinct trail behind them.

They would be easy to find.

Until it got dark.

He glanced up at the trees overhead and frowned. It was getting late, and if they didn't catch up to them soon, finding them could prove very difficult. There were a few flashlights in the group, and it would be easy enough to make torches, but then they'd be lit up targets and easy pickings. They couldn't risk that.

Their only hope was to catch them now, before nightfall, which shouldn't be difficult. After all, they were pursuing children and a man carried on a stretcher. His men were healthy and motivated, everyone

176

talking about what must be an extremely valuable artifact. Figures were bandied about, but none of it mattered. It was Dara's, so it was his. Anything they sold it for would be his, and if it were as much as his own fantasies imagined, it would be enough to set him and his loyal followers up for life in the city.

He wanted out of this hellhole. He was sick of being poor, of living hand to mouth, of being treated with disrespect. He and his friends might terrorize the village on occasion, but they had to live there, so didn't take it to any extremes—if they did, his neighbors were liable to kill him in his sleep.

He just enjoyed being a badass, a gangster, and mostly confined his true criminal activity to holding up visitors from the city or tourists stupid enough to venture into the area, lost on their way to visit where the movie The Bridge on the River Kwai took place in real life. It kept him fed and clothed, with liquor to drink, gas for his motorcycle, and money to take care of Dara.

He inhaled deeply, briefly closing his eyes as they burned with the image of her staring up at him, dying from a shot he had fired.

The life I could have given you...

He growled as he pushed through the brush, enraged that he had to be here, pursuing those responsible, rather than at Dara's side, grieving with the rest of the family. It wasn't right. It wasn't fair.

"Sir!" yelled someone from up ahead, the concern in their voice evident.

"What is it?" he asked as he headed in their direction.

"Blood!"

Zhao tensed as he quickened his pace. There hadn't been any gunshots or altercations that they had heard, so blood either meant one of his prey was wounded, perhaps from the gunfight, or something had happened to one of his scouts.

And when he saw the large pool of blood, he knew it wasn't a residual from the fight earlier.

"There's more over here!" announced Chula to his right.

"And here!"

Three pools of blood. Three scouts.

"Look for the bodies. There's no way they took them with them."

"Who?" asked Chula as he slowly spun.

"Our scouts."

Chula cursed then stepped toward a large tree, reaching down. "It's Kiet!"

Zhao spotted something odd next to a nearby tree and walked over, kicking at a pile of leaves, revealing a foot clad in a shoe he recognized. "I found Runrot."

"Here's Sajja."

Zhao cursed then raised his weapon, firing wildly into the trees ahead. "I'm going to kill you all for this!" He plunged into the jungle, roaring in rage as the others followed, the bloodlust he felt shared by everyone.

This was no longer just personal for him.

It was personal for them all.

Main Body, En Route to Kanchanaburi
Kanchanaburi District, Thailand

Leather ran ahead as gunfire startled the jungle behind them. He quickly caught up to the main group and found the five he was ultimately responsible for huddled together. Reading looked like shit, and was clearly hurting, but he was a tough old bastard who would never complain about his pain, though would never shut up about the heat.

"Is everyone all right?" asked Laura, and he had to suppress a smile, for that should be his question, not hers.

"Yes. We took out their three scouts, so they're not happy." He faced Reading. "How are you doing, sir?"

"Don't you worry about me." Reading jerked his chin toward the enemy. "What are we going to do about them?"

"I had a thought about that. Trying to move at night in this jungle is going to be difficult and dangerous, especially for us since we can't use any form of illumination without giving our position away."

Acton frowned. "I was thinking the same thing. As soon as we stop, they'll catch up to us in less than an hour."

"Try half that."

Reading sipped some water. "Do we know how many we're facing?"

"Initial count is about thirty, but more could be on the way."

Acton pursed his lips. "Guerilla tactics? Hit and run, thin the herd?"

Leather unslung the rifle and pistol he had liberated from his man and held them up. "Who wants them?"

Reading waved a hand. "Not me. I'm too exhausted to be carrying anything but my own bulk."

It was the first time Leather had heard the man admit weakness, and his clients both turned to him, concern on their faces. Acton wisely said nothing, but Laura gave the man a hug. Over the years of working with them, Leather had come to realize she thought of Reading as a father figure, and from what he knew of the former Scotland Yard Detective Chief Inspector, she was the only reason he was here.

He handed the AK-47 to Laura and the pistol to Acton, who already had an M4, then distributed the ammo appropriately. Both were excellent shots and levelheaded in combat—he had personally trained them, and had every confidence they could be trusted with weapons. "Don't shoot anything unless you're certain it's the enemy." He smirked. "Remember, a few of my guys are local."

Laura slung the assault rifle, but not before checking it, Acton doing the same before stuffing the pistol in his belt. "So, what's the plan?"

Leather walked over to a tree and snapped off a bamboo stalk about the circumference of a finger then held it up. "Get everyone with a knife to look for stalks about this thick, then start making sharpened punji sticks as they walk."

Acton eyed him for a moment then smiled. "Boobytraps."

"Exactly. If we all work together, we can be ready in about fifteen minutes to start setting some traps. I want to make it so that this jungle is so dangerous, they won't dare want to follow us in the dark."

Operations Center 2, CIA Headquarters
Langley, Virginia

"I'm sorry, sir, but I can't say who I work for. Suffice it to say that I am a friend of Dean Gregory Milton of St. Paul's University. If you have any questions, you can contact him, however time is of the essence here."

"You expect me to believe this email you sent me without any sort of verification?"

Leroux shook his head, frustrated, though not surprised at the skepticism on the other end of the line. Bunthan's father had called only moments ago, a combination of fear and anger tinging his voice as he didn't know what to believe. A man as wealthy as him probably received messages like this from time to time, perhaps all the time, but his security people likely handled them for him.

This time, they had used his direct email address, provided by Milton, and known only to personal friends. It had got the man's attention, since none of the phone calls had.

182

"Sir, have you tried calling your son?"

The man paused. "Yes."

"And?"

"I can't reach him. But that's not unusual. He's in a remote location."

An idea occurred to Leroux and he muted his headset, turning to Tong. "Get a clip of the attack on the camp. Just a couple of minutes, then send it to him."

She started working. "Isn't it classified?"

Leroux shrugged. "Everyone knows our surveillance capabilities, but lower the resolution a bit to public specs."

She smiled. "Dumbing it down."

He unmuted. "Sir, I'm going to send you satellite footage of your son's dig site under attack by the local gang."

Tong gave him a thumbs-up.

"If you check your email, you should have it now."

"Just a moment."

Leroux could hear the man working his computer, then there was a gasp.

"How did you get this?"

"I can't say."

"How do I even know this is my son's camp?"

"Check the GPS coordinates on the lower right and type them into Google. It should bring up the map showing the same geography. You can then match that to where your son is located."

More typing then a gasp. "Oh my goodness!"

"Sir, we have no time to waste. Our people are attempting to get your government involved, but aren't having much luck. Apparently, the Red Wa are involved."

"The Red Wa? Are you sure?"

"No, sir, information is sketchy, but we believe the local authorities believe this to be true, and they're not willing to get involved. At least not yet. We've only been working this problem for a couple of hours. With your connections, you might have more success."

"I can reach you at this number?"

"Yes."

"Then expect my call." The line went dead and Leroux removed his headset, tossing it on his workstation. "Well, that's done. Let's hope he has better success than we've had."

"He better," said Child, gesturing at the displays as he brought up several feeds. "I've got an unusual amount of traffic heading for that area for this time of night."

Leroux frowned. "Red Wa?"

"Either that or a Bridge on the River Kwai retrospective."

Leroux sighed. "They don't stand a chance."

Southern Gates

Ayutthaya, Ayutthaya Kingdom

April 26, 1758

Uthumphon sprinted through the southern gates, the palace guard having reported where his brother had made his escape with his personal guard and a group of friends. Word was sweeping through the kingdom that the king was dead, and that Thammathibet was now king. It was a lie, told by Thammathibet and his friends, but the disinformation was creating havoc. Already, mourners were on the street, wailing their despair at the loss of a truly loved monarch, and those in the know trembled with the knowledge of who was now king.

He had given orders to his staff to spread the word that the king was still alive, and that the rumors weren't true, but an outrageous lie was often impossible to counter without visual proof, and his father was in no condition to make an appearance on the palace balcony. But none of that mattered. His father would soon be dead, and unless he could retrieve the mask before that, he would be forced to kill his own brother.

Something he was certain he didn't have the strength to do.

The head of the king's guard, Sangkhit, flagged him down. "Your Highness, they have been spotted heading for the bridge."

Uthumphon continued down the road and Sangkhit joined him. "The main bridge or the temporary one?"

"It wasn't specified. I assumed the temporary one."

Uthumphon smiled slightly. "And you would assume that because you are aware of what is happening at the main bridge. I am quite certain my brother is not, as I have been the one running the project to repair it after the storm. If he is indeed heading for the main bridge, he will be in for a surprise."

"What are your orders?"

"Take a group to the temporary bridge. Cross it then cut off the other side of the main bridge. It is still passable, but will take time. I'll continue directly to the main bridge and trap him and his followers on it. He will have no choice but to surrender."

"Yes, Your Highness!" Sangkhit snapped orders, two dozen men splitting down an old path recently widened to carry the heavy traffic to a backup bridge built years ago, the last time the main bridge failed. Just yesterday, they had repaired the support structures for the bridge, but the wood surface that the people and carts traveled on still had a fifty-pace gap caused by the fire from at least one lightning strike during the storm. The only way to cross would be to cling to the supporting structure, a difficult and dangerous, not to mention slow, prospect.

He continued the charge, his personal guard as well as the king's surrounding him, soldiers along the way joining them as the crowds parted. Once past the new path, the crowd thinned to nothing, and he had to wonder if his brother would have questioned why. In his irrational state, however, Thammathibet might have continued on, ignoring what his eyes told him.

Whatever his brother had decided, they would soon find out. Reports were that he and his followers had passed through the gates less than fifteen minutes ago, and if they reached the main bridge, would have been forced to turn around or attempt the dangerous crossing.

An arrow whipped past and a guard cried out behind him. Uthumphon broke off the road and into the jungle as the others did the same, at least a dozen arrows clattering onto the now empty road.

"Brother! It is I! You must stop this!" he called, taking cover behind the thick trunk of a tree.

"The king is not here!" came the reply. "He is safe from you and your traitorous horde!"

Uthumphon exchanged a puzzled glance with Sangkhit. "Traitorous horde?"

Sangkhit shrugged. "I've been called worse."

Uthumphon chuckled. "So have I. By my own brother." He raised his voice. "We are not traitors, and my brother is not the king. Our father, the king, still lives."

"You lie!"

"If I am lying, why would his personal guard be with me?"

"Because they conspire with you!"

Uthumphon groaned. "This is getting us nowhere, and every moment we delay, my brother can use to cross that bridge. Once he does, there will be no catching him."

"Permission to engage?"

Uthumphon nodded. "I see no other choice."

Sangkhit turned to several of his men. "Advance through the trees, archers close to the road. Take any shots of opportunity you have. There aren't many of them, only a few dozen from what I've heard. If we kill enough of them, they may surrender."

"Yes, sir," replied the guards who broke off to relay the orders.

Sangkhit turned to Uthumphon. "I recommend you stay here, Your Highness, where it is safe."

"Very well, but if you encounter my brother, let me know. I must be the one to face him."

"Yes, Your Highness." Sangkhit headed forward at a crouch, movement on either side of the jungle evident. Too evident. He decided it was best to provide a distraction.

"Surrender now, and you won't be harmed," he called. "I know you are loyal to the king. You have simply been misled. It isn't too late for you."

"We are loyal to the king, to *your* brother. Why don't you show your loyalty to your king and stop this treasonous action?"

"The only treasonous action has been taken by my brother. It is he—"

Someone cried out, cutting him off, then a roar erupted from among the trees ahead. He peered out from behind the trunk protecting him and watched in horror as Sangkhit and the others surged from the cover of the forest, engaging the surprised group of Thammathibet's supporters blocking the road ahead. Arrows flew and swords clashed, Thammathibet's friends falling quickly, his outnumbered personal guard fighting valiantly to the last man.

But they never stood a chance.

"All clear, Your Highness!"

Uthumphon stepped onto the road and strode quickly forward, frowning at the sight before him. The road was drenched in blood, the dead and dying littering the entire area. The victors checked the enemy, slicing the throats of those that still breathed, while others checked on their own dead and wounded.

It was all so senseless.

Yet it was, unfortunately, necessary.

If only his brother hadn't acted the fool.

Sangkhit turned to one of the men. "Head back to the city. Have stretchers brought for the wounded and a crew to clear these bodies. And send reinforcements to replace our losses."

"Yes, sir!" The man sprinted back toward the city as Uthumphon picked his way through the bodies, shaking his head at the carnage, recognizing some of his brother's friends among them.

"Such a waste."

Sangkhit agreed. "Yes, Your Highness. They fought valiantly, though for what purpose?"

"They were lied to. They thought they were defending their new king. Let us not forget that when we bury them."

"Yes, Your Highness."

Uthumphon drew a deep breath as he cleared the last body and stared at the road ahead, the bridge just around the next bend, as well as the duty thrust upon him by his father.

He feared he was about to kill his brother, for things had already gone too far.

Main Body, En Route to Kanchanaburi

Kanchanaburi District, Thailand

Present Day

Bunthan carried one of the boys, whimpering with fear at the gunfire behind them, as Achara moved from child to child with Photsi, reassuring them that everything would be all right as long as they kept moving forward. Half the children were being carried now, and it was exhausting.

"Chayan!" hissed someone behind him. He glanced over his shoulder to see Acton rushing toward them holding a sharpened stick and a machine gun over his shoulder. Bunthan came to a halt and handed the boy over to one of his students who took him and continued on.

"Professor Acton. Is everything all right?"

Acton held up the stick. "No time to explain. Get everyone with a knife making these. This length, this thickness. Make sure they sharpen the tips." He indicated the children. "Make a game of it if you have to.

191

Have the kids find the stalks then the adults sharpen them. Make as many as you can in the next fifteen minutes, but keep moving forward."

Achara eyed the sharpened branch in Acton's hand. "Boobytraps?"

"Yes."

She winced. "Isn't that barbaric?"

Acton regarded her. "Do you think they're coming after us because they want to give us all hugs? This is life—"

Bunthan cut him off. "I think we understand, Professor. No need to be rude about it."

Acton handed him the stick. "I'm sorry. I'm on edge. Hugh…"

Bunthan looked back toward where the older man would be. "Is he all right?"

"I don't think he can make it. He needs to rest." Acton jabbed a finger at the stick. "Those could be the key to us surviving until morning. Get everyone on it, now."

Acton turned and ran back toward the others as Bunthan stared at the stick for a moment. History in this area had come full circle. The brutality of World War II was about to be revisited, with blood about to be spilled in the most primitive of fashions.

Main Body, En Route to Kanchanaburi
Kanchanaburi District, Thailand

Reading continued forward, his legs like lead, his chest tight. He was utterly tapped, only shame and guilt kept him moving. The distraction of sharpening punji sticks had slowed the group, and he was thankful for it. If they didn't stop for the night, there was no way he could make it.

Something was wrong.

He had assumed it was just his age. He was too old to be running from crazed criminals through the jungles of Thailand, yet it was more than that. For months now, he hadn't felt himself. Before he was diagnosed with sleep apnea and put on a CPAP machine, he had needed afternoon naps, but that hadn't been true for years until recently. The lack of energy and the lead legs he could understand since he spent too much time behind a desk, and had added ten pounds in the past couple of years.

Fifteen.

It was the pains in his chest that were new. He had never experienced angina before, but he assumed this was what it felt like. It meant something was wrong with his heart. If he were back in London, he'd see the doctor, but here, he had no options. He had to keep moving, otherwise the others would wait for him. But if he had a heart attack, and survived it, they'd insist on carrying him out.

He'd end up killing them all.

He had to lie down, to rest, but that wasn't an option. Instead, he pushed on, drawing deep breaths, struggling with his tactical breathing in an attempt to calm himself. Panic was setting in, which would only make things worse.

He was going to kill his friends.

He leaned against a particularly thick bamboo tree and squeezed his eyes shut, praying to God to get him through this so he wouldn't be responsible for the tragedy that awaited them if he slowed them down.

"Are you all right?"

He flinched. It was Mai. "Yes, just a little winded."

"I made you this."

He glanced over his shoulder and clenched his teeth tight together to prevent an outburst. Mai had fashioned him a walking stick. She handed it to him and he tested it. "Perfect height. Thank you."

She smiled then broke off a piece of bamboo that matched Leather's specifications. "I figured you could use it." She lowered her voice. "There's no shame in asking for help."

His chest ached for a new reason. "You're a wise young woman. Your father would be proud."

"I like to think so." She wiped her eyes with a knuckle. "I just hope I get to see him again."

"You will. We're going to get through this."

She sighed. "I hope so, but if we don't, at least I got to see him one last time."

Reading nodded toward Tommy. "You catch up to your man. I'll be along shortly." He held up the walking stick. "And thank you for this."

"You're welcome." She flashed him a smile then hurried on, catching up with Tommy.

Reading stepped forward, putting some of his weight on the stick, testing its strength, then, satisfied, moved on, his chest still afire, the stick helping propel him onward with slightly less effort.

Yet it wouldn't be enough.

Rear Guard, En Route to Kanchanaburi
Kanchanaburi District, Thailand

Using a combination of bamboo, paracord, and desperation, Leather created the first of what would hopefully be many bamboo whip traps. They were illegal in modern warfare, but this wasn't warfare. This was survival. They had to not only slow their pursuers, they had to convince them that continuing forward was too deadly a risk.

He tested the trap and smiled as the tripwire triggered the bent bamboo, snapping it forward, the spikes at chest height whipping with enough force to impale a man. He reset the trap then pointed at two more locations to the left and right. "Set them up there and there." He tossed the paracord to one of his men then continued forward, indicating two more places to set up traps. He wasn't too concerned with whether they were spotted, as even if no one were caught, they might still convince the enemy to stay put for the night.

Though he secretly hoped every single one of them was triggered, and every single one of them killed its target.

They were all exhausted. The children were being carried for the most part, sapping the adults' strength. Reading looked like shit, and Leather had spotted him grabbing his chest. He was concerned there might be something seriously wrong with the man, though if there were, there was nothing they could do about it except build a stretcher and carry him out.

He pursed his lips, considering the thought. The plan was to rest for most of the night if they could halt their pursuers. He had tasks for that time, but he would use some of it to fashion a stretcher for Reading, just in case. He'd carry him out himself if he had to, though knowing the man, it would be at gunpoint.

Reading was just too proud.

Leather took a knee and set to work on another trap, staring up at the canopy overhead, the light barely making it through now. The sun would set soon, then the situation's dynamic would change.

Quite possibly for the worse.

Red Wa Position, En Route to Kanchanaburi
Kanchanaburi District, Thailand

Zhao leaned against a tree, catching his breath. He was thirsty. Incredibly thirsty. He hadn't thought this through. None of them had. They had charged into the jungle thinking they would quickly catch up to their prey. After all, it was children, wounded, and academics. But he had misjudged the conditions, and they were all slowing from lack of water.

He had been stupid, and now the light was fading.

He had sent two men back to tell the new arrivals to bring water and food. He intended to press on, through the rapidly ensuing dark, and overtake the group, a group they hadn't caught sight of the entire time. The three men tracking them were dead, but they could still see evidence of the group passing through the jungle, yet they hadn't seen nor heard anyone.

It had him wondering just how far ahead they were. Surely they would have heard the children complaining by now, yet they hadn't. It had to mean the adults were motivated by more than just fear for their lives. It had to be greed. Whatever Dara had found must be worth a fortune. And it had him thinking. He wanted his revenge, he wanted them all to die, but what was more important? If they could never catch them, then he'd lose out on not only his revenge, but his prize as well.

He wanted what was Dara's.

That was all that really mattered. He wanted what was hers, and what it could do for his life. Killing everyone was just a bonus. If he could do both, then great, but if he couldn't, he had to at least come out of this with Dara's discovery. Could there be a way to end all of this right now? Could it be as simple as calling out into the jungle and stating his demands? Hand over what Dara found and you can go?

A strange sound to his left, almost like a large rubber band snapping, had him whipping around. Someone screamed in agony and he rushed toward them, gasping as he rounded a tree. One of his men was impaled through the chest, three large bamboo spikes passing entirely through him, his quivering body limp as his weight collapsed the booby trap. Several others rushed toward the death rattle when the strange sound repeated itself, another cry piercing the jungle's constant din.

"Everyone stop where you are!" he ordered as he carefully picked his way to the source of the second victim. He found another one of his men impaled, already dead, his heart punctured.

These people had no honor.

These people had to die.

Yet that might have to wait until morning, for continuing on in the dark, with the way forward boobytrapped, could prove fatal.

And he intended to survive to enjoy the spoils of the pursuit.

Main Body, En Route to Kanchanaburi
Kanchanaburi District, Thailand

Acton winced at the second blood-curdling scream, the traps they had fashioned the stakes for, doing their job. He hoped. People were being wounded or worse, dying, in an egregious fashion. Yes, it was necessary, though he was well aware of his history, and how brutal these traps were, especially during the Vietnam War. So many American soldiers had fallen victim to them that the world had agreed to make them illegal after the war ended.

Not that the world paid much attention to signed agreements.

But this was not war, it was survival, and he had no problem using them. They were protecting children here, innocents, who had done nothing wrong except have a classmate whose father was a gang member. Though there was more going on here. Why had the father shown up in the first place? Why had his daughter left the dig site?

It all had to do with the mask that Achara had told them about. Bunthan hadn't mentioned it yet, not that there had been any

201

opportunity. Little had been said in the few hours they had been moving, and he was more concerned with Reading than anything else. But he wanted to know what was going on, especially if he and those he loved could die because of it.

And he might get his opportunity soon, if Leather's plan worked.

"What are you thinking?" asked Laura as she carried a little girl on her shoulder.

"I'm thinking it's about time we found out what this is really all about."

"We'll be stopping soon. Once we get the children to sleep, you're right, we have to sit down with Chayan and get him to explain what's going on, and show us the mask."

Acton regarded her. "So, you think he has it with him?"

"If it were you, would you have taken it?"

He grunted. "Yeah, I suppose I would."

"Then don't be surprised that he has, and don't judge him either."

Acton sighed. "I hope he does have it. It could be the only bargaining chip we have."

Reading turned, the walking stick Mai had made him helping him keep pace a little better. "Bargaining chip? What are you two talking about?"

"If Chayan has the mask, we might be able to negotiate with our pursuers. They let us go, we give them the mask."

Reading's head bobbed slowly. "They might, if that's what motivates them. But from what Leather's local hires said, this guy is hellbent on revenge. He wants to kill us all because he thinks we're responsible for his daughter's death."

Laura adjusted her load. "That might have been the heat of the moment. His motivations might have changed."

"Does he even know about the mask? What Achara said about it suggested no one outside the camp knew except her."

"He might not know about the mask, but he thinks something was found made of jade."

Reading frowned. "A piece of jade? Who cares? Why would he kill over something like that?"

The boy Acton was carrying woke then squirmed out of his arms, rushing ahead to join Achara. Acton reached over and took the girl from Laura. "He's chasing an idea. To him it isn't just a piece of jade, it's something extremely valuable."

"But why would he think that?"

"Because we're here with an armed security team," replied Laura, stretching her upper body as they continued to walk. "You have to admit, it looks awfully suspicious. They find something, and a few days later a bunch of people show up with eight armed guards? That's fishy in anyone's books."

Reading sighed. "So, we created the situation."

"In a manner of speaking, I suppose."

"Lovely." Reading stopped and took another swig from his water bottle as he leaned on his stick. "You two keep going. I'm just going to rest for a bit."

"Are you sure?" asked Laura.

Reading nodded. "Go ahead, I'll be along in a minute."

Acton patted his friend on the arm and kept going, though slowed their pace considerably. There was no way Reading would catch them if they kept pace. Something was wrong with their friend, and he just prayed it was sore muscles and not anything more serious.

He would never forgive himself if his friend were to die out here, in the middle of nowhere, because he had felt compelled to come along to protect them from themselves.

Rear Guard, En Route to Kanchanaburi
Kanchanaburi District, Thailand

Leather peered through the trees, briefly catching sight of the enemy. Two were down from the traps, and the rest were holding position. An argument was underway, though without understanding the language, he couldn't be sure if it wasn't simply an excited discussion.

But every moment they weren't moving, was another chance for his people to increase the gap.

It was almost dark now, and to continue forward for any of them would be dangerous, especially when contending with boobytraps. The question was how wise were their pursuers? He had little respect for gang members. They were usually stupid, uneducated, drug addicted. Organized crime was something different. Those at the top were often brilliant, and perhaps those at the top of Red Wa were Mensa members. But not these people. These were the bottom of the barrel. They weren't thinkers, they were doers. The question was, what would they do now that they knew their lives were in danger?

205

One of them sat, then another. A lighter flashed, revealing a half-dozen were now on the ground, piling wood and leaves, a fire quickly roaring. It meant he could see them, though they couldn't see him, their vision now overwhelmed by the light.

And it meant his plan had worked—they were staying put for the night.

Unfortunately for them, he had no plans on sleeping tonight.

Main Body, En Route to Kanchanaburi

Kanchanaburi District, Thailand

Acton hid his concern with a smile as Reading groaned, lying down on the ground, his back facing the fire, his face toward a tree. He was hiding his pain, but at least now they had stopped for the night. Leather had reported that their pursuers had set up camp, and that it was safe to light several fires if needed, as his men were keeping watch while they set more traps.

Everyone was relieved, and after a quick meal, the children were down with Photsi, and the university team were settling themselves. Acton wanted nothing more than to sleep himself, but a conversation had to be had.

He sat beside Bunthan, sitting with Achara, and Laura joined him. "We need to talk."

Bunthan regarded him apprehensively as Tommy and Mai joined them. "About what?"

"About the mask."

"What mask?"

Acton steadied his anger. "Don't bullshit me, Chayan. Achara told me already."

Achara stared at her hands. "Sorry, but you were going to show them it regardless, so I didn't see the harm."

Bunthan sighed. "You're right, of course. I'm sorry. I'm just so on edge with all of this, I don't know who to trust."

Acton relaxed slightly. "Well, you invited us here because you needed someone to trust, so obviously…"

Bunthan chuckled. "Yes, I know, I know." He drew a long breath then exhaled loudly. "Do you want to see it?"

"So, you do have it."

"I couldn't leave it behind. They would have sold it off in pieces."

Laura's eyes narrowed. "Pieces? I thought it was a jade mask?"

"It's more than that." Bunthan reached over and grabbed his backpack, unzipping it. He pulled out a folded piece of cloth then unwrapped what was inside. Acton, Laura, Tommy, and Mai all gasped as the mask was revealed, the flickering firelight causing the jewels that encrusted the face to sparkle, the brilliant jade a pale representation of its true beauty only the sun could reveal with justice.

"May I?" asked Acton, holding out his hands.

"Of course." Bunthan handed it over and Acton scrutinized it using the flashlight from his phone.

"It's beautiful," said Laura. "What can you tell us about it?"

Bunthan smiled at Achara. "We believe it is the Mask of Succession from the Ayutthaya Kingdom."

Acton's head bobbed. "It certainly matches the descriptions I've read, and it is missing, but how did it end up here?"

"I'll let Achara answer that."

Achara cleared her throat. "According to our oral history, my people used to live closer to the heartland of Thailand, in the Ayutthaya Kingdom, north of modern-day Bangkok. When King Borommakot died, there was a dispute between the brothers on who should inherit the throne. The eldest brother died and the mask was lost. The younger inherited without the mask, but he couldn't hold the throne. There were too many challengers who felt he hadn't properly inherited. As you know, the kingdom only lasted another nine years after the death of Borommakot."

Acton handed the mask to Laura. "Yes, but how did it get here?"

Achara continued. "After the turmoil, my people fled the region and eventually settled here. Obviously, someone must have found the mask. They probably didn't even realize what it was, and brought it with them during the fighting."

Acton lay on his side, propping himself up on an elbow. "Then settled along the river here, and everything, including the mask, was buried during the deluge you theorized."

Bunthan nodded. "That's our working theory. I'm not sure if there's any way we can actually prove it, however."

Laura handed the mask to Mai. "How it got here is obviously of interest, but you're right, it would be difficult to prove. The fact is, however, that this is almost definitely the Mask of Succession, and that there is no way it could have reached here unless transported by hand."

Tommy refused to touch the mask. "Could it have been carried here somehow, maybe by water? You know, like it floated here?"

Bunthan shook his head. "No, the waters go the wrong direction. It had to be carried here by someone, and Achara's oral history is as good an explanation as any. When Borommakot died and his eldest son didn't inherit, no one knew why, and no one knew what happened to the mask. Since we know it ended up here eventually, that has to mean it was lost by the royal family somehow. Was it stolen? And if so, by whom? The older brother? The younger brother? Someone else entirely? And imagine if back then the same questions were being asked? Did they think the younger brother had murdered his older brother to steal the throne? And if he didn't have the mask to prove the succession had happened according to tradition, then his claim to the throne would be weak. It would explain why he only lasted three months."

Acton shook his head with a smile. "God, I love archaeology. Here we have a centuries-old mystery, something scholars have been trying to solve for generations, possibly answered by the oral history of a group of people who live nowhere near where the events happened, and a mask uncovered because of a temporary river diversion for a hydroelectric project, discovered by a little girl."

"Who's now dead," murmured Tommy.

Acton frowned. "Yes, who's now dead." He sighed. "So much tragedy over an amazing discovery. Why this world has to be so filled with greed, I'll never know."

Laura ran her fingers through his hair. "Perhaps when one has money, it is difficult to understand the feelings of those who don't. Especially in places like this."

Achara grunted. "We may be poor, but we're still civilized. There is no excuse for people like Zhao. He's a pig whether he has money or not. He belongs in prison."

Laura reached out and touched Achara's knee. "I didn't mean to imply that your people were somehow all alike."

Achara squeezed Laura's hand. "And I didn't mean to imply you did." Her hands darted to her cheeks as she shook her head. "I just can't believe this is happening. We should just give Zhao the mask and make him promise to let us go."

Bunthan vehemently disagreed as he reached out and took the mask from Mai. "Absolutely not! He would peel these gems off and sell them one by one, destroying a piece of history. Besides, he wants to kill us all. I'd rather die protecting history than die having already surrendered it."

"Speak for yourself," muttered Tommy, holding up a hand. "Sorry, but let's think about what's going on here. We've got some crazed nutbar chasing us through the jungle. He wants to kill us all out of revenge, but from what Leather told us, he's only got himself to blame. I say we hand over that damn thing that's been lost for God knows how many years, and tell him in no uncertain terms that if he continues to pursue us, the price will be far higher than he can imagine. And we make sure his men see the thing, so they know how much it's worth." He paused. "How much *is* it worth?"

211

Bunthan wrapped the mask back up. "You can't put a price on something like this."

"Bullshit. Everything has a price. Forget the history. Raw materials. How much is it worth?"

Acton shrugged. "Millions, judging by the size of some of those diamonds, many millions to a collector."

Tommy jabbed a finger at him. "Exactly! Hand that over to them, making sure a bunch see it happening, and tell them it's worth millions. They can just walk away with a guaranteed cushy future, or risk dying and losing out."

Acton pursed his lips as he thought about what Tommy was saying. As much as he hated to see a piece of history fall into the wrong hands, it was just an object. Was it worth over thirty lives? Obviously not. He was inclined to agree with the young man's idea.

"I said no!" snapped Bunthan as he returned the mask to his backpack. "In the morning we will head out and keep ahead of them like we have been. We keep setting traps, we pick them off one by one. Eventually they have to give up."

Laura leaned forward, her voice gentle. "But Chayan, you're assuming that they value life like we do. These are criminals, motivated by greed and in one case, revenge. As long as Zhao survives, and he is the leader, they will keep coming after us, and at the moment, we have no idea how many there are. We know there are dozens, but by morning, there could be hundreds."

Bunthan rose, holding the backpack close to his chest. "We're not handing it over, end of discussion." Achara joined him as he stormed off, flashing an apologetic smile at them.

"Well, that was unexpected," commented Mai.

"Agreed," said Acton. "He's too close to this. I know in the past I've been guilty of trying to protect history, but in the end you always have to balance the equation. If it were just my life at stake, I might think the same as him, but there are over thirty lives at stake, including eleven children. The idea that protecting an artifact is worth risking those lives is insanity."

Laura curled up in front of him, the fire facing her. "Well, I got the impression that Achara agreed with Tommy's idea. Let's see if she can change his mind by morning, otherwise, we might have to change it for him. Now, let's all get some sleep. I have a sense tomorrow is going to be worse than today."

Acton curled up beside her. "Let's hope you're wrong about that."

Southern Bridge

Ayutthaya, Ayutthaya Kingdom

April 26, 1758

Thammathibet stared at the vast gap in the bridge, cursing himself for forgetting about the fire that had nearly destroyed the structure, a vital lifeline for the city. When he and a few of his friends had arrived, the workers had scattered, no doubt terrified by the swords brandished by his entourage. He had sent his personal guard and most of the others back to block the road while he assessed the situation.

All he had to do was buy time. He still wore the mask, despite it being quite uncomfortable, for the moment his father died, by tradition *and* law, he would become king until the day he died. He had seen his father, and the man couldn't have much more time left. Hours at most. All he needed to do was get across this bridge, hide, then return in a few days, wearing the mask.

As king.

There would be nothing anyone could do about it, not even Uthumphon.

Swords clashed down the road and he recognized the screams of some of his friends. Aphon turned, fear on his best friend's face. "What should we do?"

"I need to get across this bridge."

Aphon gestured at the half-dozen that hadn't been sent to fight. "What do you need us to do?"

"Hold the bridge until I get across, then try to join me."

Aphon snapped out a curt nod. "You can count on us, Your Majesty."

Thammathibet shivered with the thrill of hearing the title uttered by one of his friends, and while it wasn't his yet, it would be soon.

You just need to survive a little longer.

Aphon extended a hand. "It has been a privilege to have you as my friend, and an honor to serve you as my king."

Thammathibet shook the hand, then did the same with the others. "You all honor me, and I shall see you soon."

The fighting stopped, the silence occasionally pierced by someone crying out, and he gulped with the realization it was his pursuers executing those that had survived the skirmish.

He was running out of time.

"Go!" shouted Aphon as he ripped off his shirt, drawing both his swords and taking position at the foot of the bridge. "We will hold them while you get to safety!"

Thammathibet took one last look at his friends then grabbed onto one of the thick ropes supporting the structure. He stepped onto a piece of wood extending along the side of the bridge, holding on for dear life as he made the mistake of staring down at the raging river below. If he were to fall, there would be no surviving. He crept forward, the approaching footfalls urging him on. He didn't fear they would kill him. After all, he was the eldest son of the king, even if his father didn't intend for him to ascend to the throne.

He did fear a stray arrow or jostling of the bridge that might send him to his death.

Aphon roared with a warrior's cry as good as any he had heard, and he risked a glance back to see his brave friend charge toward the approaching guards, their friends following, their own shouts joining in. Swords clashed behind him, men cried out in pain and fear, yet he continued forward, handhold to handhold, resisting the urge to check on his friends, or if he had reached the other side of the gap in the bridge.

But when the last sword clashed, the final voice fell silent, he stopped and looked back to see Aphon on his knees, his swords at his sides as his chest heaved from exhaustion.

Then Sangkhit's sword swung, severing the head of the best friend Thammathibet had ever known.

He gasped in grief as Aphon's head rolled off the road and into the brush, then another noise had his head spinning. His shoulders slumped at the sight of at least a dozen soldiers blocking his path on the other side of the bridge.

His brother hadn't made the same mistake he had, remembering the bridge was out.

"It's over, Brother."

Thammathibet turned to see his brother step past Aphon's body, slumped forward, still kneeling. "You'll have to come get me! You'll have to risk killing me if you want the mask. I only have to stay here until Father dies, then by law and tradition, I am king."

Uthumphon sighed, sheathing his sword, Thammathibet noting it hadn't been stained with blood. The coward had hung back, letting the guards do the fighting.

He's no king.

Uthumphon waved a hand at the guards. "Don't you see what's going on here? Father's personal guard is with me. They are under my orders. His wishes will be fulfilled. I will be king upon his death."

Thammathibet tapped the mask, still tied to his face. "Not as long as I have this."

"You just don't get it, do you?"

A horn sounded in the distance, several forlorn notes wailing, then repeating. The gathered soldiers on both sides of the bridge took a knee, bowing their heads. Uthumphon took a knee as well, his shoulders shaking as his chin dropped to his chest.

"The king is dead!" shouted someone in the distance, and Thammathibet smiled before remembering what that meant. He was alone. His father was gone, his mother was long dead, he was estranged from his brother, his friends massacred, and he now had the weight of a kingdom on his shoulders.

This wasn't the way it was supposed to be.

Yet nothing could be done about that now.

He stared at Uthumphon, still kneeling. "The king is dead, and I wear the Mask of Succession. By decree, I am now king!"

Uthumphon rose, holding up a hand behind him, silencing the confusion from the guards. "I'm afraid that is not to be."

Thammathibet eyed him. "What do you mean? I am your king. I wear the mask." He stabbed a finger at his younger brother. "Kneel before your king!"

Uthumphon drew his sword. "Father gave me instructions before he died. He said if I couldn't retrieve the mask before he died, I was to kill you and take it."

Thammathibet's chest tightened and his stomach churned at the words. Uthumphon couldn't be serious. Father would never order such a thing. It was inconceivable. But it was also inconceivable that his brother would lie about something like this. Could their father have ordered his execution? Was it possible? His father had always put the kingdom first. Would he, on his deathbed, order the execution of his own son simply to keep him from the throne?

Would I truly make that bad of a king?

Then he remembered his father's words.

"For the good of the kingdom, there would be only one solution."

His father had already confirmed the truth, and to order Uthumphon to kill him to protect the kingdom had to mean the man honestly did believe the realm would be harmed if he inherited the throne.

He squeezed his eyes shut, stemming the tears that threatened to erupt. His father was right. They were all right. He was by no means worthy of being king, yet, by law, he was. And as the king, he had to do what was best for the kingdom.

He had to fulfill his father's wishes.

He opened his eyes and sucked in a deep breath, then stared at his brother. "Will you acknowledge that, by tradition and law, I am the king at this moment?" His voice was calm, measured.

Regal.

Uthumphon eyed him. "Technically, yes."

"Then as king, it is my duty to do what is best for my kingdom and its subjects."

Uthumphon sheathed his sword, perhaps sensing what was about to happen. "I would agree, as would Father, I am sure."

"Then let us end this. I have never wanted to be king. You and I both know that."

Uthumphon took a step closer, his own demeanor relaxing. "Then what do you suggest?"

"I want you to be king. It's what Father wanted, and it is what our kingdom needs."

Uthumphon's shoulders slumped in relief and he smiled. "You are a wise king, Brother." He stepped to the edge of the gap. "You do know that I never wanted this? I never wanted to be king?"

Thammathibet sighed. "I know." He gave his brother a look. "Would you have really killed me?"

Uthumphon chuckled then jerked his head toward Sangkhit. "No, but he would have."

Thammathibet laughed then smiled at his brother. "I will pledge my allegiance to you until the day I die, and will at least make a sincere attempt to not make life too difficult for you."

Uthumphon grinned then stepped back from the gap. "How about you come over here and we'll end this, then go home and prepare for Father's funeral. Together we will reunite our family, and it will be stronger than ever."

Thammathibet agreed then tentatively stepped back toward his brother. Swords were sheathed around them, bows slung, arrows returned to their quivers as he made his way back to safety. The horn continued to sound in the distance, and his chest ached with the knowledge that his last interaction with his father had been so horrible. They had argued, he had pulled a blade on his own blood, then brought shame to the family.

Uthumphon stepped closer, wrapping his wrist around one of the ropes then extending his other hand. Thammathibet reached out to take it when the mask slipped slightly. He gasped and grabbed it with his free hand, pressing it against his face as his heart pounded. He glanced down at the furious waters below as he adjusted the fit.

"Give me the mask," said Uthumphon, his concern evident.

Thammathibet shook his head. "No, it's still tied. It just shifted, probably from all the sweating." He took another step and the mask slipped down his face to his chest. He grabbed at it once again, but this time with the hand gripping the rope instead of his free hand.

"No!" cried Uthumphon as he surged forward, his hand extended in front of him. He dove toward Thammathibet as he tumbled off the edge of the bridge. Thammathibet stretched out his hand and cried in relief as Uthumphon caught him, abruptly halting his fall. "Hold on! I've got you!"

Thammathibet checked to see that the mask had merely slipped off his face and was still tied around his neck. He stared up at his brother, then saw the horror in his eyes as Thammathibet's sweat-soaked hand slipped in his brother's grip.

"Help me!" shouted Uthumphon, and footfalls pounded on the bridge, out of sight. But they were too far away, and his hand was slipping rapidly now.

He met his brother's gaze one last time and grabbed the mask with his other hand to pass it up to him, when the grip was broken.

"Forgive me, Brother!" he cried as he plunged to the raging waters below, the sounds of his brother's scream drowned out by the crashing rapids.

And in an instant, the last king of Ayutthaya to inherit the throne through the passage of the Mask of Succession, was dead.

Leroux's Office, CIA Headquarters

Langley, Virginia

Present Day

Leroux yawned then rolled off the couch in his office, a room he rarely saw these days. Most of his time was spent in an operations center, which was fine by him. He preferred the action to paperwork. He rubbed his eyes then flinched to see his girlfriend, CIA Operations Officer Sherrie White, sitting in his chair, smiling at him.

"Well, look who decided to join the land of the living."

He yawned again then checked his watch. It was approaching morning in Thailand, and Acton's last text message indicated they were settling in for the night, so he had ordered his team to get some rest while a backup crew monitored things. The fact he hadn't been woken meant the night in Thailand had been unremarkable. "When did you get here?"

"A few hours ago."

His eyebrows shot up. "You've been sitting there watching me sleep for that long?"

She laughed. "Don't be so full of yourself. I was here for a briefing. I'm leaving tonight for Moscow, remember?"

"Oh, yeah, I forgot. Sorry."

"No worries. I'll be back in about a week, but comms should be decent so you might hear from me. If not, don't worry. I can take care of myself."

"Yeah, well, just be careful. Things are pretty tense in Russia these days."

"Well, that's why I'm going. We need to identify people willing to deliver the bullet should it become necessary."

Leroux plopped into one of the guest chairs. "Well, let's hope it never comes to that."

"What, you don't think he should die?"

"Oh, he should die, but his own people have to do it on their own. If one of our contingency plans has to do it, that means this thing has gone nuclear."

"Yeah, I suppose you're right." Sherrie gestured toward the couch, her eyebrows bobbing suggestively. "Time for a quickie?"

"You know we can't do that here."

She sighed then rose. "I guess you're right. I'll just go to Russia to seduce all those men who have access to their president, all horny because my—"

"Very quick!" He leaped from his seat and locked the door as Sherrie squealed in glee, ripping her clothes off.

The phone on his desk buzzed.

"Don't answer that."

Leroux gave her a look. "I have to. I'm on duty." He picked it up and found his backup on the other end.

"This is your wake-up call."

Leroux laughed. "Thanks. I'll be there in ten"—Sherrie flashed ten fingers twice—"better make that twenty minutes. I need to freshen up."

"Okay, see you then."

He hung up and was mauled.

Russia didn't stand a chance.

Main Body, En Route to Kanchanaburi

Kanchanaburi District, Thailand

Reading had pretended to be asleep through last night's conversation between the others. He had intentionally not gone to the bathroom before heading to bed, as he wanted to wake up through the night so he could decide what to do. Unfortunately, he had slept longer than expected, though from what he could tell, he was the first awake.

He sat up and stretched. His entire body was aching, though that was expected after what he had slept on, and all the walking from yesterday. He took a slow, cautious breath and could still sense a hint of the chest pain he had fallen asleep with. It would be back with a vengeance in no time, he was certain.

According to Leather's briefing on their situation last night, if they could maintain the same pace as yesterday, they could clear the jungle and reach Kanchanaburi by nightfall. Texts from Milton indicated their CIA friends were involved, and some members of Bravo Team were inbound. If everything went smoothly, then the authorities might

225

already be on their way, perhaps shaving hours off the time they would have to keep ahead of their pursuers.

But only if they could keep pace.

And there was no way he could.

He squeezed his eyes shut, fighting back a wave of self-pity. This was no time to lose it. This was the time to accept reality, and reality was that he was a liability. He was the oldest here by fifteen years, but beyond that, he had a health issue that would take him out if he tried to do all day today what he had done yesterday for only a few hours.

Then they would have to carry him, assuming he survived.

He wiped his eyes dry as he pictured his son. He would kill to talk to him right now, to say goodbye, but that wasn't in the cards. He glanced to his right to see his friends, still asleep, and wished he could say goodbye yet he couldn't—they would never let him do what he had decided to do.

He rose, as quietly as he could, then crept over to where Bunthan was sleeping. He gently lifted the backpack containing the mask, then set out to either put an end to this, or at least buy those he loved some time.

It had been a good life, a full life, with few regrets. And if he were to die today, this would be how he would want to be remembered.

Sacrificing himself to save the innocent.

Rear Guard, En Route to Kanchanaburi

Kanchanaburi District, Thailand

Leather peered through the dense trees, watching for any movement. The sun was about to rise, and they would be underway soon. And so would their pursuers. He hadn't heard any commotion yet from the enemy camp, which meant they hadn't discovered some of his team's handiwork.

Six more were dead.

They had picked them off in the middle of the night, sneaking into their camp and silently eliminating them then taking their weapons and ammo. They now had eight more guns to arm the civilians, and scores of rounds. Unfortunately, they hadn't taken out Zhao as he was too close to the fire and surrounded by his men.

Killing him might have put an end to this.

A sound to his left had his head spinning and his eyes narrowing. Someone was heading toward the enemy camp. It couldn't be one of his team, as only three of them were awake, the others catching some

227

rack time, the switch-off having just happened. Could it be one of the enemy? He squinted at the shadow and rejected that possibility. Whoever it was, was far larger than anyone pursuing them. This was no Asian gangbanger.

It had to be Reading.

What the hell was he doing? Was he sleep walking? He drew his flashlight and flicked it on, aiming it directly at Reading, and suppressed a gasp as it glinted off something gripped in the man's hands that had to be the mask he had heard about. Reading spun toward him and waved him back before continuing forward.

It was clear now what was going on. Reading was going to give Zhao the mask and try to make a deal to let the rest go. It was suicide. Especially after what his team had done to their ranks overnight. At least eight of the enemy were now dead if those caught in the traps were counted, not to mention at least half a dozen killed or wounded in the initial encounter.

And Zhao's daughter, Dara.

He wanted to stop the man, but it was too late. He was almost at the enemy encampment, and Reading was liable to run from him, raising the chances he might trip one of the traps. His current path, if he stayed on it, should be clear, and chasing him could have him changing course.

He had to let the man go.

He executed a birdcall and stepped into the open, his two men acknowledging the signal, falling back with him.

Someone shouted and Leather said a silent prayer for the brave bastard, doing this because he knew he couldn't make today's journey.

And wanted to save his friends.

If you survive this, we're coming back for you.

Red Wa Position, En Route to Kanchanaburi

Kanchanaburi District, Thailand

Zhao leaped to his feet and spun in a full circle, searching for what had woken him. The camp was stirring, and several people were now shouting, but he couldn't make out what was going on. It was still dark and their fires were mere embers, nobody having stoked them through the night.

"He's dead!" shouted someone. Zhao spotted someone kneeling, shaking a prone form that didn't stir.

"Sonchai's dead! Someone slit his throat!" cried another one of his men.

Zhao grabbed his AK-47 and fired several rounds in the air. "Everybody calm down! Stoke the fires! We need light!"

Wood was tossed on the three fires and within minutes, an orange glow was cast over the entire area, six bodies discovered at the periphery. Their enemy had been here in the night, had raided their camp, had killed his men. A shiver ran down his spine as he realized he could have been killed just as easily as any of the others. He had no desire to die. He wanted to live, to get whatever treasure had been found by Dara, and to live the life he was always meant to live.

Difficult with a slit throat.

"Is anyone missing?" he asked, the numbers appearing smaller than he remembered the night before.

"I don't see Thahan. Thahan are you here?" asked one of his men.

There was no response.

Another name was called out and he held up a hand. "Figure it out then let me know!"

The men huddled together as he stared at the dead. Sentries had been posted, but they had obviously fallen asleep. Or had they? The bodies were at the edge of camp. Had the sentries been killed? He didn't know who was on duty through the night, only who was when he fell asleep. They were supposed to switch off, but no one was to disturb him.

Chula walked over. "Boss, it looks like six dead and five missing."

"Five missing? Were they taken?"

Chula shook his head. "I don't think so. According to the guys, the entire last watch is gone. I think they left."

Zhao growled. "Cowards! Why would they leave? We're so close to victory."

Chula shrugged. "I don't know. Maybe they found the dead and got scared."

"And didn't wake us?" Zhao spat. "I'll kill them myself when we get home."

A twig snapped and everyone spun. Zhao raised his weapon as a large white man stepped into sight, the fire highlighting his frame.

And the most incredible mask Zhao had ever seen.

Dara's treasure.

Main Body, En Route to Kanchanaburi

Kanchanaburi District, Thailand

Leather cautiously entered the camp, making certain the sentry posted spotted and recognized him. He headed directly for the professors and took a knee, gently shaking Acton then Laura. "Professors. Wake up."

Acton flinched, bolting upright and reaching for his weapon, Laura doing the same. Leather reached out, blocking them both from arming themselves.

"It's Cameron. Stay calm."

Acton rolled to his knees and stretched. "My God, Cam, you're going to give someone a heart attack one of these days."

"Sorry, sir, but we've got a problem."

Laura rose. "Are they coming?"

Leather stood and extended a hand to Acton, hauling him to his feet. "They might be, though I'm not sure. Something has happened."

Acton obviously sensed his tone. "What's wrong?"

"Hugh took the mask and just walked into the enemy camp."

233

Laura gasped as they spun toward their friend's sleeping place, finding it abandoned. "Why would he do such a thing?"

Acton skipped the reason. "We have to get him."

Gunfire rang out, a single burst of several rounds, stirring the entire camp.

Leather ignored it. "There's no way to get him. If they don't have him already, they will any moment now. He's obviously going to try and negotiate with them. Give them the mask in exchange for letting the rest of you go."

Laura's eyes glistened in the slowly growing light. "Why would he do that?" She gripped Acton's arm, burying her head in his chest.

Acton wrapped an arm around her. "I got the sense something was wrong. He didn't seem himself. He was really struggling." He tossed his head back, groaning. "He must think he's going to hold us up. He's doing it for us, the crazy bastard."

Tommy and Mai rushed over. "What's going on?" asked Mai.

"Hugh took the mask and went to the Red Wa camp."

Mai yelped, covering her mouth. "Why?"

"He must have overheard our conversation last night." Tommy grabbed at his hair. "This is all my fault. If I had just kept my mouth shut—"

Acton shook his head. "No, it's not your fault. We were all thinking the same thing, regardless. You just had the balls to say it first. If you hadn't, I would have. Hugh's a grown man. He makes his own decisions." He turned to Leather. "What can we do?"

"We can't risk a rescue. They'll kill him the moment we try. We have to hope his plan works. I'll stay behind to see what happens to him, while the rest of you take advantage of whatever delay this might buy us. If he does succeed, and they head back, I'll come let you know."

Acton shook his head. "You stick with him, but don't risk your life. If they're going to kill him…" He couldn't bring himself to finish the sentence, and Leather understood why. This was one of Acton's best friends, and he was effectively telling him to let the man die.

"I understand, Professor. Let's hope it doesn't come to that." Leather gestured at the camp. "I suggest you get everyone moving as quickly as possible. If you can keep pace, you'll reach the town before nightfall. If they choose to follow after getting the mask, then that means they are determined to kill everyone. No matter what, you have to reach that town tonight. After what we did to them overnight, they won't risk waiting again until tomorrow morning."

Laura eyed him. "What did you do overnight?"

Leather decided details were best left for his after-action report. "You'll read all about it when this is over. For now, just know that they're going to be pissed."

"The mask!" cried Bunthan, scurrying about, searching his sleeping area. "Someone took the mask!"

Leather stabbed a finger in the man's direction. "And get control of him. The last thing we need is that idiot trying to get the mask back."

Acton agreed. "We'll take care of him. You go take care of Hugh."

"I'll do my best."

235

Leather headed back toward the enemy, and his hopeless task. There was no way they would let Reading live, and after what his team had done overnight, his final moments might be brutal. And that begged the question he dreaded to answer.

Would he need to put a bullet in the man to save him from an agonizing death?

Red Wa Position, En Route to Kanchanaburi
Kanchanaburi District, Thailand

Reading slowly stepped into the firelight, his hands raised, the mask held out in front of him as their pursuers reacted. As he had approached, what sounded like panicked confusion had ruled their camp until a burst of gunfire then some yelling brought it to a halt. He had chosen that moment to make his presence known, rather than walk into chaos.

Guns were turned on him and he stopped, his hands still up. "My name is Hugh. I'm a guest of Professor Bunthan's. I've come to talk, and have brought the mask."

A man rushed forward, an AK-47 gripped in his hands, rage on his face. He slammed the butt of the rifle into Reading's stomach, doubling him over, then ripped the mask from his hand, holding it high as he shouted something in triumph, those around him cheering, some shooting their guns into the air as Reading fell to his knees, forgotten. His heart hammered as his chest tightened, and he struggled to control his breathing before pushing back to his feet—he couldn't risk staying down, for in a situation like this, it was too much of a temptation for his opponents to lay a beating on him.

He stood in silence as the celebration continued, taking the opportunity to survey the situation. There were half a dozen prone figures lying at the outskirts of several fire pits. There was no way they were sleeping through this, so he had to assume they were dead. Leather and his team had evidently been busy through the night, and that could prove a problem.

These men were angry.

And perhaps even scared.

Would they take out their frustrations on him before he could negotiate for his friends' lives? He had already handed over his only bargaining chip, though perhaps that wasn't necessarily true. Their lives were a bargaining chip. If they had lost men to the booby traps, then another half-dozen overnight to Leather's team, they had to realize the danger. Keeping going could mean death, and for what? Revenge? The mask meant a future, and he had to convey that to them.

If they gave him a chance.

A shout from their leader had everyone calming down then turning to face Reading. The man stepped forward, shaking the mask, rage in his eyes. He said something that left Reading wishing he spoke Thai.

"I'm sorry, I don't understand. I only speak English."

"Why you bring this?" asked the man, his English broken, his accent thick.

"A peace offering."

"What you mean?"

"Are you Mr. Zhao?"

The man nodded.

"This is what your daughter, Dara, found. We want you to have it. What happened should never have happened. Professor Bunthan should never have lied. The people you are chasing, the children, his guests, his staff, had nothing to do with this, and didn't even know what he had done. I'm asking that you take the mask, which as you can see is worth *millions* of American dollars, and leave this place in peace. We will leave and never return."

Zhao's eyes had flared at the mention of the mask's value, and whispers rippled through the crowd as what was said was translated for those who didn't speak English. Most eyes were now on the bejeweled artifact, rather than their prisoner. But not Zhao's. "You killed my daughter! I must have my revenge!"

Reading had to be careful here. The report he had heard was that Zhao, or one of his men, shot Dara, yet he couldn't say that. "I don't know who killed your daughter. In the heat of battle, things happen that no one means. I'm certain that whoever shot your daughter never meant to, and feels horrible about it. They will be haunted for the rest of their days with that memory." He could see the bloodlust in Zhao's eyes, yet it was clear there was torment behind them—but this man needed his revenge. "If you require revenge, then I"—he drew a breath, holding it for a moment—"I offer myself."

Zhao rushed forward, tossing his rifle aside and drawing a long machete from his waistband. "I will have my revenge, old man, and when I'm done, you'll regret ever setting foot in my country!"

And with those words, the machete was drawn across Reading's chest, slicing through his clothes and skin, and he roared in agony as he sacrificed himself for his friends, his eyes clamped shut as a life well lived played out, ending with his son, whom he wouldn't get to say goodbye to.

And his damaged heart broke.

Main Body, En Route to Kanchanaburi
Kanchanaburi District, Thailand

Laura cried out in anguish at their friend's horrifying scream. She collapsed into James' arms and he held her tight, the two of them trembling as another cry brought the surrounding jungle to a brief halt, as if all life within the sound of Reading's agony knew a life was about to end.

And for what?

A trinket.

Yes, the academic in her knew it was more than that, that it was a priceless artifact, yet it was still just an object, assigned value by man and history.

It was not worth dying for.

But that wasn't why Reading was dying. He wasn't dying for an object, he was dying for those now standing in silence, in respect, for a man most of them hadn't known before yesterday, to whom most hadn't said two words since their plight had begun.

A man who was the best of them.

Achara stood nearby, tears flowing as her head sagged, but Bunthan muttered something in Thai, still stomping about in a rage over the fact Reading had taken the mask. He snapped something and Achara gasped in horror.

James let her go and turned to the couple. "What did you just say?"

Bunthan glared at him. "I said it serves him right! He had no right to steal the mask!"

James charged forward and clocked the selfish piece of shit on the chin. Bunthan dropped like a sack of potatoes and James dropped to a knee, raining blow after blow on the man's face before stopping himself, his chest heaving from the effort. He jabbed a finger in Bunthan's bloody face. "That man is dying to save your pathetic ass. If I ever hear you say another disrespectful word about him, I'll beat the living shit out of you again. Understood?"

Bunthan stared up at him in horror but said nothing.

"Understood?" repeated James.

Bunthan nodded then James rose, walking back toward Laura as Achara and several of Bunthan's students rushed toward the felled professor.

James took her hand. "I thought you were going to stop me."

Laura grunted. "You're lucky you did it first, otherwise his new girlfriend would have had to watch him get his ass kicked by a woman."

James wrapped an arm around her shoulders and squeezed as another cry from their friend reminded them why what had just happened was so necessary.

A man was being tortured to death to save their lives.

And there was nothing they could do about it but take advantage.

Laura clapped. "Let's move, people. He's doing this for all of you."

Bags were grabbed and tears wiped as everyone headed out, a long day of travel ahead of them if they hoped to reach the town before nightfall. And with each step, Laura's tears continued to flow, as did her husband's, as the cries of their friend faded into the distance.

And she swore every last one of those responsible would die when this was all over.

Operations Center 2, CIA Headquarters

Langley, Virginia

Leroux stared at the displays as he entered the operations center, a smile on his face, a spring in his step. He checked his happiness slightly as he spotted Tong, aware of the torch she continued to hold for him, and not wanting to rub his joy in her face. "Report."

"Mostly bad news, I'm afraid," replied Tong.

Leroux tensed as he sat at his workstation at the center of the room. "What's happened?"

"We just received a text update. Reading took the mask into the hostiles' camp. He's been captured and is being tortured."

Leroux closed his eyes for a moment, saying a silent prayer. Reading was a good man, loyal to a fault. For him to do this meant he could see no other way out of this, and that wasn't good. He was an experienced soldier and police officer, and understood tactical situations as well as the mindset of the criminal element pursuing them. If he believed this was the only way, then he must not have had confidence the civilians could reach safety before they were caught.

But to die in this way?

He shuddered.

"Understood," he said quietly as he opened his eyes. "What else?"

"Our people are underway. They think they can reach Kanchanaburi by nightfall."

Child grunted. "Yeah, only if those assholes don't catch up to them."

"If they're lucky, Reading's sacrifice will buy them the time they need," said Tong.

"Or the reprieve," added Leroux. "He has to be thinking they'll give up on the pursuit if they have the mask."

Tong frowned, jerking her chin toward the displays. "I don't get the impression that's going to be the case."

Leroux faced the screen and his eyes narrowed. "What the hell am I looking at?"

"Probably the first traffic jam this area has ever seen. We've got cars and motorcycles from the entire region converging on that dig site."

Leroux's heart sank. Red Wa was exercising its muscle, likely to send a message to the population that if you messed with one of their families, you died. His understanding was that the gang leader had accidentally killed his own daughter, but that wouldn't be the story that had gone out. The story would have been that one of Leather's team had killed her in cold blood for no reason, and that revenge was demanded.

The mask was now irrelevant.

"How many?"

"It's not clear. At least a hundred. They've been heading directly into the jungle as they arrive."

"I assume armed?"

"From what we can tell, all of them."

Leroux sighed, his shoulders slumping. "And we're sending three guys. Status on Niner and the others?"

"They've landed and have rendezvoused with our local contact. They'll be in the area shortly, but I'm not sure what they can do."

Leroux tapped his chin as he thought of Reading. "I can't send three guys against a hundred-plus, but there won't be any stopping them." He pursed his lips. "Let's keep them heading into the area then we'll decide what to do." He paused. "You said, 'mostly bad news.' Does that mean there's good news?"

Tong smiled slightly. "Yes. Bunthan's father just notified us that the Thai Army is now involved. They're moving troops into position in Kanchanaburi. They should be there in the next few hours."

Child spun in his chair. "And what are they going to do? Just sit there and wait for our people?"

Leroux stared at the displays. "Let's hope not. If they leave Kanchanaburi and enter the jungle to meet up with our people, they might just stand a chance."

Red Wa Position, En Route to Kanchanaburi
Kanchanaburi District, Thailand

Zhao stepped back, their prisoner having passed out yet again. As satisfying as this was, it was taking too much time. He still wanted his revenge, though as he caught his breath and refocused on what was going on around him, second thoughts clouded his mind. They had Dara's treasure, a mask so incredible, it had to be worth millions like their prisoner had said.

And it was a perfect wealth delivery system. Each gemstone was worth a fortune, and he could simply pry them loose with his knife, selling them one at a time as he needed funds. He would have to, of course, share some of this wealth with the men, but as their leader, it was expected he'd keep the lion's share.

Then a thought occurred to him. What of Red Wa? He had dreamed of becoming a full-fledged member, but now that he knew his fantasies over what Dara had found were real, and not only real but beyond his wildest dreams, did he need them anymore? This mask

247

could fund a lifetime of debauchery in the city. They would likely demand he hand over the mask as an entry fee, then relegate him to running the region he already commanded.

It wasn't fair.

And he'd be damned if he let them take what Dara had found.

He had already paid too high a price for her discovery.

He regarded his prisoner, still unconscious, his shirt drenched with blood as he hung from his arms, bound to a tree. He'd live for days if allowed to, and his torture, along with the monetary rewards that would flow from the mask, would be enough to quench the bloodlust.

It would have to be.

This pursuit was over.

He eyed the others, still excited about the mask, greedy glances directed at it when they thought he wasn't looking. This was worth too much. It was too tempting. Loyalty meant nothing when wealth like this was at stake. If he weren't careful, his men could turn on him. Life meant little in these parts, and they wouldn't hesitate to kill him if they thought they could get away with it.

He beckoned Chula over, the only one in the group he truly trusted. "What do you think?"

Chula glanced at the prisoner. "I say kill him, go home, and end this."

Zhao's eyes darted toward the others. "What about them?"

Chula wisely kept his eyes directed away. "I think they're a little too excited about what Dara found."

"So, you think someone might make a play for it?"

"Yes."

"So do I." Zhao scratched his chin. "And if Red Wa finds out, they'll want to keep it for themselves."

"I agree. What do you want to do?"

"We need to even the odds."

"You mean…"

"You and I are the only ones walking out of this jungle."

Leather watched from his hiding place, the last man left behind besides Reading. He had sent the rest of his team on with the civilians with instructions to maintain the buffer they had already established. Over half an hour had passed since Reading had been captured, and he was confident the group was well underway. The longer Red Wa delayed their pursuit, the more likely the others would reach Kanchanaburi first.

The question was, what was going on? He could see Zhao and one of his men holding a whispered conversation while the others excitedly talked among themselves. He was close enough to see glances at the mask, still gripped in their leader's hand, and he recognized greed when he saw it.

If Zhao wasn't careful, he might have a mutiny on his hands.

At least no one is paying attention to Hugh.

His plan was to track Reading for as long as he was alive, and for the moment, the heaving chest confirmed, despite the torture he had suffered, he was still alive. He could see only three scenarios playing out. One was that they killed him now, another that they left him there to deal with upon their return, and finally the third, unlikeliest but

249

preferred option, they took him back to their home base to hold for ransom.

If they chose the first option, there was nothing he could do. The numbers were too great. The second, depending on how many they left behind to guard their prisoner, might give him the opportunity for a rescue, though carrying the big man through the jungle for ten or twenty hours would be brutal and slow, leaving the risk of capture.

But the third gave a tantalizing number of options.

The fact Zhao hadn't killed Reading yet suggested he wanted more time with the man to continue to make him suffer, or was planning on the ransom route. If he had to guess, if Zhao realized the true value of the mask now in his possession, he would forget about any ransom, since it would pale in comparison to the street value of his prize.

Zhao picked up his AK-47 sitting against a tree as his partner unslung his own weapon. They both faced Reading, their guns aimed at the former detective's chest, and Leather said a silent prayer, thanking the man for his sacrifice, and God for the end to his suffering.

Then both men spun around, opening fire on their own, mowing them all to the ground.

And Leather smiled.

Greed had won out.

Main Body, En Route to Kanchanaburi
Kanchanaburi District, Thailand

Acton grabbed two of the children, hauling them onto his shoulders then sprinting ahead with the others as sustained gunfire rattled in the distance. He had a distinct impression that the earlier shots were celebratory and from the same location. If correct, it meant their enemy hadn't yet continued their pursuit.

And perhaps that Reading had successfully negotiated their safe passage.

If their friend had saved them, the question was what was happening to him. He had heard the man's screams, and for Reading to cry out in agony like that, whatever they had done to him had to have been truly horrific. Acton knew no man stronger than his friend. His eyes watered as he thought of Reading, and he pictured the first time they had met in the basement of the Triarii headquarters in London.

It seemed a lifetime ago.

251

And at this moment, fleeing from an enemy hellbent on killing them all, part of him wished for the simpler times before any of them had met. He was a professor at a small university known to few, with a low-budget dig in Peru, without an enemy or care in the world.

Yes, life would have been simpler if he had never found that crystal skull that had set everything into motion, but if he hadn't, he never would have met Laura, they never would have met Bravo Team, Tommy and Mai, or Reading. Though as he pictured what could be happening to his friend, he realized that if Reading had never met them, he'd still be working for Scotland Yard, doing the work he loved with his best friend at the time, Martin Chaney, at his side.

What a cruel world.

The gunfire stopped and everyone calmed slightly. He put the children back on the ground and they sprinted toward Achara nearby. He smiled at Laura. "I'll try not to take that personally."

She grunted. "You should have seen how quickly mine bolted." She glanced over her shoulder. "I can't get Hugh out of my mind."

"Me neither. Part of me hopes he's dead so they can't torture him anymore, and part of me hopes he's still alive so we can stage a rescue." He sighed. "I just don't know what to do."

She took his hand and he felt her body shaking. He stopped, taking her in his arms, and held her tight as his own tears flowed. Somebody hugged him from behind and he checked to see it was Mai. He extricated an arm to include her when Tommy joined them, and the four of them held each other, crying for their friend.

And he prayed that his sacrifice was worth it in the end, and that these children were saved because of it.

Please, Lord, take care of our friend.

Red Wa Position, En Route to Kanchanaburi

Kanchanaburi District, Thailand

Zhao kicked the body of a man who until minutes ago he called a friend. Yet with the money he now had, he could buy new friends who wouldn't expect a share of the profits, just the perks of association. Chula fired a round into a survivor's chest.

"I never liked him."

"Who?"

"Chakan."

"Yeah, he was an asshole but his sister was hot and willing."

"He never knew about you two?"

Zhao shrugged. "If he did, he never said anything."

Someone crashing through the jungle, from the direction of the dig site, had them both taking cover. He aimed his weapon, unsure of who to expect, when one of the men he had sent back for supplies last night, Chaloem, emerged from the trees, coming to a halt at the edge of the massacre.

"What the hell!"

Zhao stepped out from his cover, stuffing the mask under his shirt. "It just happened."

Chaloem stared at him, his mouth agape. "Are they all—"

"Dead?" finished Chula as he stepped into sight. "All but us."

"Who did—"

"The enemy," said Zhao. "They surprised us in our sleep, murdered the sentries, then slaughtered the group before they had a chance to defend themselves."

Their prisoner groaned and Chaloem's eyes shot wide as he finally spotted the man tied to the tree behind Zhao. "Who's that?"

"We captured him before he could escape."

Chaloem's eyes narrowed. "But I just heard the gunfire. How did you have time—"

"Enough questions!" snapped Zhao. "Report!"

Chaloem flinched but complied. "Red Wa is here. They answered your call and are here to avenge the death of your daughter by the hands of foreigners and agents of the government."

"How many?"

"At least a hundred. They're just behind me."

As if to confirm the report, the sounds of more arrivals approached. Within moments, they were joined by several others he didn't recognize, all coming to an abrupt halt at the sight of the bodies.

"What the hell happened here?" asked one of them.

Zhao stepped forward. "They surprised us in our sleep."

The man cursed. "How many did you lose?"

"Almost thirty."

The man spat. "Unacceptable!" He eyed Zhao then Chula. "Which one of you is Zhao?"

Zhao stepped forward as more men arrived. "I am."

"And it is your daughter that was murdered?"

"Yes."

"My boss wants you to know he grieves with you and your family, and that it is clear this region needs our protection. You now all work for us, and you are regional commander. What are your orders?"

Zhao's entire body tingled. This was what he had always wanted, and now his dreams were coming true. He pointed in the direction of the enemy. "They're heading for Kanchanaburi. Kill them all. No exceptions."

The man sneered. "Consider it done." He charged into the jungle with the others, and Zhao watched as scores of warriors, now under his command, followed his bidding. He indicated for Chaloem to go with them, and when the last of them rushed past, he turned to Chula with a smile. "We did it."

Chula shook his hand. "You did it, boss. How's it feel?"

"Damn good."

Chula gestured toward the mask stuffed inside Zhao's shirt. "And what about that?"

Zhao lowered his voice. "That, my friend, is *our* little secret." Their prisoner groaned again and Zhao faced him. "Now, what do we do with you?"

"I say kill him. We don't need him anymore, and with Red Wa here, they'll avenge your daughter."

Zhao's head slowly bobbed as he approached the man, hanging from the tree like the Christian Jesus. Red Wa was delivering vengeance for him, and with him having given the order, it was as if by his hand. Yet it wasn't satisfying enough.

Several men entered the camp and Zhao turned to them. "I am Zhao, regional commander. Do you recognize my authority?"

"Yes, sir!" they shouted in unison.

Zhao pointed at the prisoner. "Make a stretcher and bring him back to the dig site. I'm not finished with him."

"Yes, sir!"

Machetes were pulled, including his own, and as the new arrivals set to work cutting down bamboo to fashion a stretcher, Zhao ran his blade once again over the man's chest. "I'm not finished with you yet. Not by a long shot."

Main Body, En Route to Kanchanaburi
Kanchanaburi District, Thailand

Other than Reading's attempt to save them, the hours so far had passed relatively uneventfully. Bunthan and his people were giving Acton and the others a wide berth, and Acton had to admit he felt a little bad about punching the man. He had lost control over words and shouldn't have. When this was over, he'd apologize, no matter how much it might turn his stomach.

After all, he only felt a *little* bad.

Leather's local contact, Vidura, rushed up to them, something he had been doing every hour. "How is everyone doing?" he asked, slightly out of breath.

"We're making good progress," replied Acton. "Nobody is falling behind, and the men are frequently alternating on the stretcher. How are your men? Any word from Cameron?"

"Negative, and I'm taking that to be a good thing."

Laura regarded him. "What do you mean by that?"

258

"If your friend is dead, the colonel would rejoin us. As long as he doesn't, he's either dead, or your friend is alive. I'm betting on your friend."

Acton pursed his lips. "Let's hope you're right."

"Any sign of Red Wa?" asked Tommy as he and Mai joined them.

"We can hear them. They're pushing forward, and it sounds like in greater numbers. We've still got about half an hour on them, but two hours ago that was an hour. They're catching up, and doing it quickly, but they're fresh, so should start to tire. We've also been setting up boobytraps, and occasionally we can hear one tripped, so that's making them a little more cautious. If we hadn't, they'd have already caught you."

Acton frowned. "And here I thought we were making good time."

"The children are slowing you down, and so is the stretcher."

"We've been carrying the children when they get tired, but it ends up exhausting the adults too. Do you have any idea how much progress we've actually made?"

"I had one of my guys climb a tree and get a good GPS fix. We're over halfway there. If you keep this pace, we should reach Kanchanaburi by nightfall."

Laura checked her watch, something that made Acton slightly envious as he rubbed his bare wrist. "That's eight hours from now."

Vidura shook his head. "Six. Nightfall is earlier in the jungle. Remember, you can't see a thing here once the sun reaches the horizon. They'll be forced to stop again."

"And so will we," muttered Tommy.

Acton agreed. "He's right, and we have to assume they know that, so they'll keep after us. If in two hours they gained half an hour on us, then that means they'll probably catch up to us in another two. Even if they tire and you buy us some time, we're looking at maybe three or four hours tops. That's a hell of a lot shorter than six. I don't see how we can get to Kanchanaburi before they get to us."

Vidura smiled slightly. "I hate it when clients can do the math." He sighed. "You're right, Professor. Unless something drastic happens, they *will* reach us."

"Then what?" asked Laura.

"Then we make our final stand. Every one of us fights to the death while the teachers continue on and try to save the children."

Acton stared up at the heavens and closed his eyes. "Lord, please help us, and if not all of us, then the children, for they are innocent in all of this."

Laura took his hand and squeezed it gently. "Amen."

En Route to Kanchanaburi, Thailand

Niner, Atlas, and Jimmy rode in the back of what was the prettiest helicopter Niner had ever seen. Shiny, new, plush leather, in-flight entertainment systems. It was something he could imagine the professors leasing them to go into war.

But their ride wasn't courtesy of the professors, it was their new boss—at least according to their revised covers. When they had landed in Bangkok in the middle of the night, they had been met by a local contact that was most definitely CIA. They had been taken to a hotel, briefed, and fully equipped.

They were loaded for bear, and on hold. A chopper was arranged for a morning insertion into the area, however Langley didn't want them going in alone—there were estimated to be over 100 hostiles after the professors and their people. Niner didn't like the odds, but he'd rather get his ass in there and do some damage, perhaps buy them the time they needed to make their escape on foot.

Three highly trained, properly equipped Delta operators could do a lot of damage in the jungle against what sounded to him like a bunch of untrained gang members who only shot their AKs in the air when Doogie Howser came on, and fired their pistols sideways like their favorite gangsta rapper.

Easy pickings with camouflage, night vision, and precision weapons.

They could thin that herd to half inside of ten minutes.

The problem as he saw it was getting into position. They had no idea where in the jungle the two parties were, except that everyone was heading generally south, and the professors were ahead of the bad guys. By how far, no one knew, and a helicopter insertion through a thick canopy was dangerous at the best of times, and they could drop right into the middle of the enemy.

Easy pickings.

But things had changed by morning, when they received a visit at the hotel from the man now sitting across from him, and the owner of the helicopter.

Chao Fah Bunthan, the father of the archaeologist in charge of the dig, and a man who might even be richer than the professors.

"Five minutes!" announced the pilot over the speakers, and Niner and the others began checking their equipment.

Chao Fah leaned forward. "Just remember, you're part of my private security. The Army knows you're coming, but they don't know who I suspect you really are."

Niner smiled slightly. "And who do you suspect we are?"

Chao Fah regarded him. "Son, the moment I heard what was happening, I had my people pull everything they could on your Professors Acton and Palmer, and they found out a lot of interesting things. I don't suspect I know who you are, I *know* who you are. However, let's pretend I don't so you can all maintain your covers. What's essential here is that my government contacts believe you are hired guns. Mercenaries. If they think American Special Forces are operating on Thai soil without approval, there'll be hell to pay, as you Yanks might say."

Niner was impressed. The man's intel gathering capabilities were obviously good, though a lot of what he said could simply be supposition based upon stories from conspiracy websites.

After all, they weren't always complete bullshit.

Even the weather report was correct from time to time.

"You've got an Asian, a Black man, and a dude as white as snow. I think they'll believe we're mercs."

Atlas agreed. "We just need to make sure we don't appear too professional. Discipline issues, attitude problems."

Jimmy grunted. "With you two, that shouldn't be a problem."

Atlas eyeballed him. "What's that supposed to mean?"

"What do you mean what do I mean? You two on a mission with BD or Red in charge is bad enough. With no one in charge? It's going to be a gong show."

Niner tapped his chest. "I'm in charge."

Atlas turned to him. "What makes you think that?"

"Because it was my phone they called. You two just happened to be scarfing down my grandma's noodles at the same address."

Chao Fah stared at them all, his mouth slightly agape. "Are you three for real?"

Niner grinned at him. "Just getting into character, sir. We'll be fine."

"I hope so." Chao Fah raised a finger. "And just to clear things up." He tapped his chest. "*I'm* in charge."

Khwae Noi Tributary Dig Site

Kanchanaburi District, Thailand

Zhao was exhausted, though he suspected those who had been carrying the ridiculously heavy prisoner were even more so. It had taken hours to retrace their steps back to the dig site, and he found it transformed. The road along the riverbed was packed with cars and motorcycles, and a few Red Wa members milled about. There were girls everywhere, perks of being part of Red Wa, and if he weren't on a mission, he'd be sampling the goods from the city.

Instead, he made a beeline for his motorcycle, still parked by the large tent. He turned to Chula, indicating their prisoner. "Have him brought to the clubhouse. Bring him around the back. I don't want anyone seeing him being brought in."

"I'll take care of it."

Zhao started his bike then gunned it up to the road before stopping in front of a group of girls, one of them particularly gorgeous. "I'm Zhao. Red Wa regional commander. Get on the bike."

The girl smiled and climbed on, holding him tight as he cranked the throttle, sending them surging toward town. He was exhausted, and he wanted a woman to clean him up, give him a massage, then make him forget his worries for a while.

There'd be plenty of time for the prisoner tomorrow.

Outside Kanchanaburi

Kanchanaburi District, Thailand

Niner stood with the others, assessing the situation through his ballistic sunglasses, his expression serious. There was no joking around, at least for the moment. Chao Fah was talking with the scene commander, a Thai lieutenant colonel who was all smiles and handshakes.

"It must be nose planting season in Assland," observed Jimmy.

Niner agreed. "Yeah, I looked this guy up on the way to the airport. He's mega-rich. Like billions."

Atlas grunted. "If my daddy had billions, I don't think I'd be playing in the dirt looking for antiques. And I certainly wouldn't be in the middle of nowhere without significant security."

"Apparently, the father has only paid for his kids' educations, and that's it. It's up to them to earn their own billions."

Jimmy's eyebrows rose slightly. "That's kinda cold."

Atlas shrugged. "Not really. It makes them be better people, I would think. I'm sure there's a safety net, like right now, if things go wrong. I mean, how many kids get themselves into trouble and Daddy calls in the military?"

"I don't know about the military, but my dad would call in Local 342. Those dudes would bust some skulls."

Chao Fah beckoned them over and they joined their "employer" and the Thai commander. "This is Lt. Colonel Kim. He's in charge of the operation. Colonel, I've brought these men in as observers. I hope you don't mind but I've equipped them, just in case."

Kim eyed them, hiding his displeasure well, instead giving a curt nod. "As long as they stay out of the way, they are welcome to come along."

"Excellent," said Chao Fah. "They'll be my eyes and ears." He shook Kim's hand once again. "Good luck, Colonel. I won't keep you any longer. Please go save my son and the others before it's too late."

"You can count on us, sir." Kim turned on his heel and walked away, joining a group of his officers nearby. Chao Fah faced Niner and the others.

"Do you need anything from me?"

Niner responded. "No, sir. We have everything we need. We'll join the colonel's men and advance with them. I'll report back to you as soon as we know anything."

"Thank you." Chao Fah lowered his voice. "If you can't save my son, kill as many of those bastards as you can."

Niner checked his response. "We'll do what we can, sir. Remember, we're not actually mercenaries. We have our own mission."

Chao Fah frowned. "You're right, of course."

"Don't worry, sir. Our mission aligns with yours. We're here to help save all of them, including your son."

Chao Fah nodded. "Good luck." He headed for the helicopter and the pilot powered up the luxury beast.

Niner pulled out his phone and called Leroux's direct line. It was answered immediately. "This is One-One. Sitrep?"

"Nothing new from Professor Acton since the morning update where he reported Agent Reading having surrendered to the hostiles with the mask. Judging from the GPS fix from that message, and the rate we believe they're traveling at, we estimate five miles between them and your current position."

"Any indication of the enemy position?"

"Negative. For all we know they could have overtaken our people already, and that's why we haven't heard from them."

Niner frowned. "Let's hope that's not the case. Anything else we need to know?"

"Not at this...just a sec." The line went silent for a moment before Leroux returned. "We just got some good news. We have footage of Reading being brought on a stretcher to the dig site. It looks like they're loading him into a car."

Niner pursed his lips. It was good news that the man was alive, but he might not be for long. "Track him and arrange helicopter transport for us from here. I want to be able to move on a moment's notice."

"Understood."

"Keep me posted. One-One, out." He turned to the others. "Reading is alive."

Atlas smiled. "When do we go get him?"

"As soon as we've made sure the others are safe."

"Good idea," said Jimmy. "If we went off and saved him, and something happened to the others, he'd kill us."

Khwae Noi Tributary Dig Site
Kanchanaburi District, Thailand

Leather squatted at the edge of the tree line, keeping out of sight as he assessed the situation. Zhao had just left with one of dozens of prostitutes or groupies, leaving his men to deal with Reading. The man was lying on the makeshift stretcher used to carry him out of the jungle, and the men responsible for carrying the heavy load were all lying on the ground, exhausted, as some of the women brought them food and water.

The other lone survivor from the earlier massacre hit the ground the moment his boss' motorcycle was out of sight, and was gulping down water, wisely avoiding the beer the others were drinking. The dig site had been turned into an outdoor party, likely prepping for a bash after the men returned from their hunt. At the pace he had seen them moving through the jungle, he had little doubt they would overtake his people if they slowed. These new arrivals were fresh, prepared, and didn't have the dark to contend with like the others had last night. They

271

had already caught up to their comrades shortly after the slaughter, and would be pressing forward quickly.

But that wasn't his concern anymore. Vidura and the others would deal with it, hopefully with help from Langley. His lone concern now was Reading. One of the girls was giving him some water, which was a good sign in two ways—he was alive to drink it, and they intended to keep him that way.

At least for now.

Leather took the opportunity to drink some water and eat some rations while deciding what to do next. He couldn't stay here, as he might be discovered at any moment. His best bet was to use the trees as cover and head toward the village. Reading would either be kept here, or moved, and the only road from here went through the village center. With Langley involved, he had no doubt they knew Reading was here, so tracking him was no longer his concern.

Being in position for a rescue was.

Main Body, En Route to Kanchanaburi
Kanchanaburi District, Thailand

Acton pressed forward with a child in each arm. His muscles ached, his entire body screaming for relief. But this was it. This was the end. Sporadic gunfire behind them from weapons he recognized as a mix of what he would expect Red Wa to be using and what he had seen held by Leather's team, indicated a firefight was taking place. Tommy estimated they still had two miles to go. At their pace, that was almost an hour. There was no way they could keep ahead.

They had to make a stand.

"Tommy!"

Tommy stopped. "Yes, sir?"

Acton handed him one of the children. "Take her." He flagged down one of Bunthan's students. "Take him." Freed of his burden, he turned to the others. "We have to delay them. I'm going to join Leather's team. You guys keep going."

"Bollocks!" Laura smacked her AK-47. "I'm staying with you."

273

Mai's eyes flowed. "But you'll die!"

Acton smiled at her, though his chest ached. "Don't write us off just yet. The most important thing is saving those kids. I'm counting on you two to make that happen. No matter what happens, no matter what you hear, you keep running. Save yourselves, and when you get a chance, you call Greg and tell him what happened. If we buy it here, I want a damned big memorial service."

Laura elbowed him. "Make mine a more intimate affair."

Mai swatted her, sobbing. "Stop joking!" She threw herself into Laura's arms and Acton embraced Tommy then Mai.

Acton pushed them away. "Now go, and don't look back!"

They both reluctantly turned, taking the little girl with them. Acton readied his weapon and spotted Bunthan nearby with Achara. He had to tell them what was happening. He strode over, Laura behind him, and Bunthan flinched as he spotted him.

Acton held up a hand. "I'm not going to hit you. I'm sorry about that."

Achara frowned. "He deserved it for what he said."

Bunthan flushed, ashamed that the woman he cared for wasn't on his side. "She's right. I shouldn't have said that. You didn't have to hit me so many times, though."

Acton agreed. "You're right, I shouldn't have. You said something in the heat of the moment, and I did something in the heat of the moment. Listen, I'm apologizing." He extended a hand. "Truce?"

Bunthan shook it. "Truce." He sighed. "And more. You've gotten us this far. I don't know what we would have done without you and your wife and team. I'm just gutted that your friend did what he did for no reason." He jutted his chin toward the oncoming Red Wa. "They have the mask and they still want to kill us."

Acton's stomach churned with the thought his friend's sacrifice had been for nothing. "He still bought us time. We're about an hour away from the city. You're in charge now. Get these people to safety, okay?"

Bunthan stared at him, puzzled. "What do you mean?"

"We're going to stay behind and fight. We'll delay them as long as we can. Every minute we buy is a minute closer to safety."

"I can't let you do that. It's my responsibility."

"There's no time to argue. We're trained. The ammo and weapons are better in our hands than yours. You two know where you're going. Get them to safety."

Bunthan's eyes glistened as Achara wept. "I don't know what to say. It's been a privilege knowing you both." He smiled wryly. "Despite the beating."

Acton laughed and slapped the man on the shoulder. "Go." He turned, ending the conversation before it delayed them any longer, and headed toward the gunfire with Laura at his side. His heart ached, and a lump formed in his throat as he looked over at Laura, charging toward the danger with him.

Please God, if one of us lives, let it be her.

Rescue Party, En Route from Kanchanaburi

Kanchanaburi District, Thailand

Niner pushed through the jungle, the bamboo thickening the deeper they went. He had been in environments like this before, and never enjoyed them. Heat, humidity, bugs that were bigger than they had no business being, and thousands of living things that only wanted to kill you.

Like Detroit on a Friday night.

"My ancestors may have come from the jungle, but this boy is not happy to be back," rumbled Atlas.

Jimmy glanced at him. "I don't think your ancestors were built like a tank. They probably had an easier time moving through shit like this."

Niner gripped one of the trees. "Do they have bamboo in Africa?"

Atlas eyed him. "Do I look like an encyclopedia?"

"You don't want to know what you look like."

"Watch your mouth, little man, or I'll snap you like one of these bamboo shoots."

Niner continued forward, shaking one of the trees. "These things are pretty tough. I don't know if you could snap them."

"I only have to snap you."

Gunfire ahead had them pausing, including the Thai with them. The colonel signaled for the advance to continue and the soldiers moved forward, this time at a quicker pace. Niner sprinted ahead, determined to close the gap as quickly as possible as Leather's team wouldn't be firing at nothing.

It meant Red Wa had caught up to the professors.

"Friendlies on your six!" announced Acton as he approached Vidura from behind.

Vidura didn't bother looking, instead pointing to his left then right. "Find cover and pick your targets! Take two shots then fall back!"

"Copy that!" Acton broke right and Laura left. He slammed into a tree then peered out, his weapon at the ready, and gulped. Dozens if not scores of Red Wa were advancing, and as each came into sight, the muzzles of their assault rifles flashed, sending lead across the battlefield, blasting apart the bamboo around them.

Those behind them didn't stand a chance if this line of defense broke.

He picked a target and fired, the man dropping, clutching his stomach, then he took out another before turning and running at a crouch to another thick tree behind him. He glanced to his right to see

277

Laura falling back with the others then lost sight of her. He took up position and again picked a target, squeezing the trigger once, then taking out another that crossed into his sights.

Someone got a bead on his position and a sustained burst of gunfire had him crouching, covering his head as the tree he hid behind shredded. He hit the ground and crawled on his belly, abandoning his position, and made for a nearby stump. He rolled to a knee and fired two more rounds, taking out two more of the enemy, but there were just too many. They had obviously just encountered the quickest of the bunch, and as the rest caught up, it became clear they were facing at least one hundred men.

There was no way they could win this.

Achara cried out as she stumbled and fell. Bunthan skidded to a halt and rushed back to help her up as the gunfire became a sea of white noise behind them, so many guns firing he could no longer pick out the individual weapons. His entire body shook with the sobs of what he had done, the guilt and shame of everything that had happened over the past few days, overwhelming. He wanted to die with the others, to stand and fight, not out of a sense of duty or bravery, but because he didn't want to live with what was to come.

He was pathetic.

He helped Achara to her feet and they continued forward as the children screamed around them. The terror they must be feeling, his students and staff must be feeling—it was all his fault. He glanced at Achara. What she must think of him. His pathetic display this morning, his unforgivable words. He didn't deserve a woman like her, and she was too good a person to abandon him under these circumstances.

And the moment they were safe, she would leave him. Of that, he had no doubt.

But there was no way they were surviving. They still had a mile to go, and the gunfight was so close, he was surprised stray bullets hadn't whizzed by them yet. All they could do was keep moving forward.

And pray the heroes sacrificing themselves survived long enough to make a difference.

Niner heard them first. Or at least that's what he would tell anyone who asked him to recount today's events. He held up a fist and they came to a halt as the Thais continued forward. "Do you hear that?"

"Children?" asked Jimmy.

Niner smiled at them. "Children!" He charged forward, making a beeline for Kim. "Colonel!" The man looked over and Niner held a hand to his ear then pointed ahead. "Children screaming!"

Kim cocked an ear then gave a thumbs-up, shouting something in Thai, hopefully a warning to his men to hold their fire. Niner directed his weapon at the ground as he continued forward, and cried out with joy as he spotted someone carrying a child burst through the trees ahead. The young man came to an abrupt halt, terror in his eyes as the soldiers continued their advance. Kim shouted something and the relief on the man's face was obvious, though the young girl he was carrying didn't share it. Niner passed them, anyone behind them now safe. More appeared, and he signaled for Atlas and Jimmy to split off. "Look for our people!"

His friends spread out along the line as the Thais pressed forward, over a dozen civilians now behind them. Niner kept a mental count of the children as he spotted them, and was up to six when he recognized Bunthan from his briefing notes.

"Professor Bunthan!"

The man glanced over at him as he helped a young woman, struggling with what might be a sprained ankle. "Yes?"

Niner joined them. "I'm a friend of Professor Acton. Do you know where he is?"

The man suppressed a cry of despair and squeezed his eyes shut before he finally managed to deliver the devastating news. "Him and Laura and the guards, they're…they're the ones fighting. You have to help them before it's too late!"

It was all Niner needed to hear. He continued forward and spotted Atlas with Tommy and Mai, and said a silent prayer of thanks that they were all right.

But he had friends to save, and no time to waste.

Acton scrambled on his hands and knees, taking up position behind a tree already occupied by Vidura as the enemy continued to advance, pouring a steady wall of lead at them. They had to have taken out at least twenty if not thirty, but Red Wa continued to press their advantage. He had spotted two of Vidura's men go down, along with one of Leather's.

And he hadn't seen Laura in minutes.

"Good to see someone's alive still," said Vidura.

"Likewise."

Vidura leaned out and took two shots, Acton doing the same. Vidura cursed. "I'm out."

Acton pulled out his last mag and handed it over. "That's all I've got left."

"Then let's make them count."

Laura cried out to their left and Acton paused. "You okay, babe!"

"Just a graze! I'll live!"

"Yeah, but for how much longer," muttered Vidura as he fired two more rounds.

"Long enough to kill a few more of these bastards." Acton fired another round but was forced to duck back behind his cover before taking a second.

"Ah shit, they've made our position."

Gunfire poured on the tree, the thumping vibrations shaking Acton's back. This was it. There was nowhere to run to, and he only had half a dozen rounds left. They were about to be overrun, and he had no desire to be taken prisoner. He reached over and slapped Vidura on the back. "It's been an honor."

"The honor's been mine, Professor."

Acton jumped up and sprinted toward where he had last heard Laura. He spotted her lying prone behind a tree, and for a moment thought she was dead before he noticed she had her pistol out, firing at the approaching onslaught. He dove over her and took up position on the other side of the tree she was using for cover.

"I figured if we're going to die, we should die together."

Laura fired again then flashed him a smile. "We're not dead yet."

"Wait for it." Acton squeezed off another round as Vidura fired to their right. He glanced over at her, searching for her wound, but couldn't find it. "Are you hurt?"

"Just grazed my thigh. Should leave a sexy scar."

"If you're thinking we've got time to bring sexy back, it's going to have to be the quickest of quickies. One for the record books."

She fired twice. "You mean like that time in Paris?"

He groaned. "Our last seconds together, and you have to bring up my most embarrassing sexual moment?"

She fired again. "Yeah, 'moment' would be how I'd describe it."

He fired his last rounds and flipped over onto his back, pressing up against the tree. "Hey, I would think you'd be flattered that I found you so hot I…well, you know."

She fired again then rolled over, sitting up beside him, all their ammo spent. She took his hand and squeezed it. "It *was* flattering." She rested her head on his shoulder and he wrapped his arms around her.

"I love you. More than I've ever loved anyone."

"I know." She looked up at him, tears filling her eyes as the gunfire continued to tear the jungle apart around them. "You're the best thing that ever happened to me."

He wiped the hair from her face. "There better be a Heaven, because this can't be it. There's so much more I wanted to do with you." He squeezed his eyes shut and his entire body shook as he gave in to the realization that the wonderful life they had only just begun to build was over, and that they had failed to buy the others the time they needed to reach safety. "I'm so sorry."

She sniffed. "You have nothing to be sorry for. It's been an amazing life."

"Stay down!"

Acton opened his eyes and saw a blur rushing toward them. He wiped his eyes dry with his knuckles and gasped as the massive Atlas, flanked by Niner, Jimmy, and scores of Thai soldiers ran past them, opening up on the enemy. He struggled to get to his feet when a meaty palm reached over and shoved him back into the ground.

"I said, stay down!"

Acton rolled over and saw that their three friends had taken up position around their tree as the Thai soldiers continued forward.

"Their line is breaking!" reported Jimmy, and within minutes, the gunfire had faded enough for Atlas to stand.

"Are you two okay?" asked Niner.

"Laura's been shot."

"It's just a graze."

Niner dropped beside her. "Why don't you let an expert decide. Where?"

She tapped her right thigh and Acton noticed the blood for the first time.

Niner grinned at her. "Well, darlin', I'm finally going to get to say to you what I've been dreaming of saying for years."

Acton eyed him. "And what's that."

"Take your pants off."

Red Wa Clubhouse, Muban Chong Sadao

Kanchanaburi District, Thailand

Zhao rolled from the bed with a smile on his face. It was the same old shitty house he had lived in for years, but this clubhouse, as he and the guys had taken to calling it, was now officially a Red Wa clubhouse. He leered over the naked body in his bed and smiled. The women were already better.

He was going to love being regional commander.

He had wanted to escape this shithole of a town, but that could wait. He had power now, and with the official backing of Red Wa, he'd have the respect he deserved from those who had always treated him like dirt.

This town was going to pay.

But there was work to do. He and Chula had killed their entire crew to preserve the secret of the mask. It was a heavy price, and he did feel bad about it, but it was kill or be killed. If he hadn't done what he had, one of them, if not all, would have betrayed him.

285

It had him wondering whether he could truly trust Chula.

He had grown up with him, and he was his best friend. Had always been. And if you were going to be rich, what was the point without real friends? He wanted to enjoy his life, and to do that, he needed Chula.

He'd let him live.

As long as there was no hint of potential betrayal.

As soon as things calmed, he'd break down the mask and start selling off the gemstones. But he also needed to get the mask to a safe place in case the authorities came here. With Red Wa's connections, any raid on the house should come with plenty of warning. He was protected now, and Red Wa's tentacles ran deep throughout Thai law enforcement.

He was safe now.

Yet that didn't mean he could be stupid.

He pulled on his pants and headed down the hall. He opened the door to Chula's room and found his friend lying on the bed with three honeys, all naked.

Life is going to be unbelievable.

He continued down the hall, finding the others that had helped carry their prisoner out of the jungle, scattered about, all with women of their own.

If even the minions can have women like this, I'm going to live like a king!

He found their prisoner tied to the showerhead in the bathroom, the tub stained with his blood. He smacked the man. "You alive?"

The man groaned. He was alive, but barely. He had planned to have some fun with the man today, but there was no time for that. He hadn't heard anything yet about what had happened with the pursuit after leaving. Surely if Red Wa had caught up to the city folk, he would have heard by now, though perhaps not. There was no phone service, so they might have to make their way back, and could have camped overnight after slaughtering their prey.

Last night had been a good night. He was clean, the massage he had received was probably the best he had ever had, and the sex was definitely far above par. He was in a good mood. He was Red Wa, a regional commander, and unbelievably wealthy—or soon to be.

It was time to start being smart about things.

And that meant killing his prisoner, getting rid of the body, and finding a safe place to hide the mask.

He pissed then headed down the hall, searching for a machete.

The kill had to be silent.

Niner crept forward, approaching the clubhouse, if you could call the dump that, from the rear. Atlas was with him, and Jimmy was covering the front with Leather. Half a dozen Thai Special Forces covered the other two sides as a major force held position outside of town, awaiting the all-clear before sweeping in to round up the Red Wa scattered throughout the area, most still at the dig site.

Nobody wanted to do anything that would risk Reading's life.

Assuming the man was still alive.

Langley had followed the vehicle used to transport Reading here, confirmed he was alive when brought in the house, and that he hadn't left. As far as they could tell, there were six hostiles inside, and at least

J. ROBERT KENNEDY

as many women. The women were being treated as victims, however any of them could turn on them at any moment, so the orders were to shoot to wound if possible, kill if necessary.

He didn't want to shoot women.

"I've got movement at the three-four corner," reported Atlas.

Niner adjusted his scope and spotted a man rummaging for something in a back room. It was the first movement they had spotted since they got into position five minutes ago, and it signaled an impending change in the dynamic.

With one up, the entire house could wake in moments.

"Move in," came the report over his earpiece, the Thai commander finally giving the order.

Niner and Atlas surged forward. He had to be first inside. There was no way he wanted to risk a stray bullet killing the man they were here to save.

Reading flinched, the nightmarish scenarios playing out in his head finally, mercifully, ended as he woke. It took him a moment to reorient himself through the pain. His arms were stretched out above him, and he could feel his hands bound to something overhead. The weight of his entire body tortuously pulled on his wrists, elbows, and shoulders.

But it was nothing compared to the pain in his chest.

The slices through the flesh were bad enough, and he had spotted bone, he was certain, when they were carrying him out of the jungle. The pain from his heart had settled during that journey, as it was the other bastards that had to physically exert themselves. He had taken those hours to calm his breathing and focus on resting. The brief respite at the dig site, where one of the young women had given him food and water, had been welcome. It had helped him regain his strength, but that had all been sapped overnight as his captors had hung him like a piece of meat.

He was ready to die.

He wanted this over with. His friends were either alive, perhaps thanks to his efforts, or they were dead along with the children and others. If the former, then he could die knowing he had sacrificed himself for something worthwhile, and if the latter, then he didn't want to live.

He just hoped Spencer would understand.

He was a good boy. A smart boy. Reading just hoped he would somehow know the truth of what had happened here these past two days. But if his friends were dead, then there would be no one to tell of what he had done, and his son might bury his father thinking he had been a coward, surrendering to the enemy.

He squeezed his eyes shut and gasped as a stabbing pain pierced his chest. This was beyond anything he had experienced so far, and it had to be it, the big one he had heard about.

He stared up at the heavens, his eyes welling.

"Take me now, you bastard. You owe me at least that much."

A sound, metal scraping on concrete, forced him back to reality. He turned his head and spotted Zhao standing in the doorway, smiling, a long machete in one hand.

"Time to die, old man." He stepped forward, the blade's tip leaving a thin trail in the floor. "Try to be quiet, won't you? I wouldn't want to wake the neighbors."

"Why don't you go fu—"

Something shattered the window and Zhao jerked back. There was an ear-piercing bang and a blinding flash that overwhelmed Reading's senses. He slumped, his wrists screaming in agony as shouts erupted all around him. Gunfire rattled throughout the house, but it was all a fog as his heart raced, palpitations overwhelming him, then a jolt fired up his arm and into his jaw.

And his world slowly faded to black as what was happening around him gave him hope. If they found him, then maybe they had saved the others.

And he could finally die in peace.

Bumrungrad Hospital

Bangkok, Thailand

Reading stirred to the sounds of hushed whispers and beeping machines surrounding him. He kept his eyes closed for a moment as he struggled to remember what had happened. Then it came rushing back and one of the beeps increased rapidly.

Someone took his hand and squeezed. "It's all right, Hugh, you're safe."

It was Laura. He opened his eyes and everything was a blur. He blinked a few times and her smiling face came into focus. "Oh, thank God!" he whispered, the effort to speak surprisingly difficult. "Jim?"

"It takes more than hundred to three odds to take me out, buddy." Acton came into view, his smile welcome.

"Tommy and Mai?"

"We're here, Hugh," came Mai's voice from his right.

"The children?"

Acton patted him on the shoulder. "You saved them. You saved them all."

Someone cleared their throat. "I like to think we had a little something to do with it."

Reading smiled as he recognized Niner's voice. "I've got a million questions—"

Laura placed a hand on his chest. "And I'm going to answer them all, but how about I save you some time. First, let me tell you that you're going to be all right, and the doctors say you'll make a full recovery. In fact, you're probably going to be feeling a lot better than you have been in years."

Reading's hand reached for his heart. "My heart. Did I have a heart attack?"

"Yeah." Niner appeared to his left, along with Atlas and Jimmy. "When we hit the house they were keeping you in, you went into cardiac arrest. Luckily the Doc told us you were having chest pains, so we brought a defibrillator along with us, and I'm a gifted and handsome medic—"

"What's handsome have to do with it?" asked Atlas.

"Just laying the groundwork for who plays me in the movie. Anyway, as I was saying, we zapped you back to life, got you on the chopper, and the doctors here took a look at you."

Laura continued. "You had a 95% blockage in one of your arteries. They put a stent in, and you'll be as good as new."

Acton stepped aside as a nurse came in. "You'll feel like shit for a while, not because of the procedure, but because of the heart attack and the fact you had a shitload of amps run through your body. Not to mention the work they did on your chest with a machete. But the docs said you had minimal damage and should recover."

Laura pressed Reading's hand to her lips. "And if you want, you can recover at your new home with us."

Acton leaned in. "And we'll hire you a nurse to change your diapers."

Reading's eyes shot wide. "Diapers?"

Everyone laughed and the nurse admonished them all. "Don't aggravate the patient!"

Acton backed off. "Yes, ma'am."

Reading turned to the nurse. "Is it all right if we put the bed up?"

"Yes." She handed him the control and pointed to the correct button. He pressed it and the head of the bed slowly rose, revealing everyone in the room.

He smiled then choked up.

Laura placed a gentle kiss on his forehead. "Thank you for what you did for us."

"Yes, thank you," said Acton. "And if you ever do anything that stupid again, I'll kill you myself."

Reading chuckled. "Well, if this stent does what you say it will, you might not have to worry about that. I might be brave, but I'm not stupid. I just knew there was no way in hell I could keep up." His eyes widened. "Wait, what happened to the mask?"

"They found it when they raided the house. It's now at the university, safe and sound."

"And everyone else? Cameron and his team?"

Acton frowned. "Cam's all right. He tracked you and kept watch the entire time. He's with his man in the burn ward downstairs. He'll recover, but he'll have some scarring. Vidura survived, but everyone else was killed, unfortunately."

Reading sighed. "What a waste. And Red Wa?"

Niner gave the update. "The Thai Army swept through the entire area after you were rescued, and arrested everyone that didn't belong there. It'll probably take them a week or two to sort it all out, but let's just say Red Wa no longer has a presence in that village."

"And thank goodness for that."

Everyone turned to see Bunthan enter the room with Achara, holding hands. He appeared to have taken one hell of a beating from someone, and it raised scores more questions in Reading's mind.

Bunthan stepped forward, extending a hand. "I just wanted to thank you personally, sir, for your sacrifice. What you did saved us all. On behalf of myself, my students, and my staff, you have our undying gratitude."

Achara stepped closer and smiled. "And on behalf of myself, Miss Photsi, and my students, I'd like to thank you as well." She held up a large piece of cardboard. "The children drew you this."

Reading teared up again as he examined the card, not understanding a thing on it, everything written in Thai. But he hadn't seen anything more beautiful in years. "Thank them for me. It will go up on my wall at home." He squeezed Laura's hand. "My new home."

A tear rolled down her cheek.

Reading gestured at Bunthan's face. "What ran into you?"

Acton shifted uncomfortably, as did half the room.

"Umm, let's just say I was delivered a well-deserved message."

Reading's eyes narrowed and he was about to ask for a better explanation when Acton interrupted. "Sometimes some questions are better answered at a later time."

"Or never," muttered Laura.

Reading, ever the copper, noticed Acton's knuckles and made eye contact. Acton clasped his hands behind his back, answering the question for him. "Huh, I look forward to hearing the whole story one day."

Niner slapped him on the leg. "Bah, why wait. You did some stuff, they did some stuff, we did some stuff. The important thing is the job is done, we're still on vacation, and we can still make dinner at my grandma's if we leave now."

Atlas grinned, patting his stomach. "Yeah, that's all I needed to hear. Glad you're going to be all right, Hugh, and I'd love to continue the convo, but there's Korean barbecue that needs eatin', and I'm starving."

"Keep your hands and feet away from his mouth, ladies and gentlemen," said Jimmy. "Nothing is safe when this man is hungry."

Hugs and handshakes were exchanged, and the three Delta operators left the room. Laura turned to Bunthan and Achara. "So, what's next for you two?"

They both flushed and turned slightly away from each other, though still held hands.

"I mean with the dig site."

Bunthan cleared his throat. "Umm, well, my father has agreed to fund it and provide a security team. We'll be going back in a few days."

"And the mask?" asked Acton.

"It will be studied, then put on display for the public to see. Fortunately, it's still intact. Zhao never got a chance to break it apart."

"Thank God for that," sighed Laura.

Reading grunted. "I don't know what's so special about that thing. You know, it's incredibly uncomfortable."

Bunthan, Achara, Acton, and Laura all stared at him, a little too intently.

"What do you mean?" asked Bunthan.

"Well, I tried it on as I was heading to Zhao's camp. Just out of curiosity."

Acton bowed deeply then turned to Laura. "My dear, put out the fine china. We have royalty staying at our humble abode."

Reading eyed him. "What the devil are you talking about?"

Laura curtsied. "He who first wears the mask after the death of the king, is the king until the day he dies. You are now the king of Ayutthaya. Congratulations, Your Majesty."

North of Ayutthaya, Ayutthaya Kingdom

May 5, 1758

Phong tugged on his fishing net, his heart leaping at the heavy load. Things had been slow in recent days, barely catching enough to feed the family let alone barter for goods they needed. But if the heft he now dragged to shore were any indication, the dry spell might just be about to end. He pulled the net onto the shore, gripping it over his shoulder, then turned to see his prize.

And gasped.

Among the fish flopping on the rocks was a man, clearly dead for days. He stepped forward and flipped him over onto his back and gasped at the terrifying mask the man wore, scurrying back several paces before he caught himself. He chuckled with embarrassment, then glanced about to make certain no one had witnessed his foolishness, finding himself alone as he expected.

He approached the body again and poked the man with his foot several times. He was definitely dead. Phong scratched his chin, uncertain as to what to do. The body should be dealt with, but he didn't have the time nor inclination to take care of it himself. He examined the clothing, and kneeled beside the man, touching the soiled tunic. It was smooth, unlike anything he had ever felt. He reached forward to remove it then thought better of it.

Even the dead deserved respect.

But not his time. It was growing late, and he was already overdue. The fish he had managed to catch would feed the family tonight, and there were a few extra that they could trade in the village just upstream. He stared at the body. He couldn't just leave him there. It would attract wildlife, and perhaps ruin his favorite fishing hole.

He said a silent prayer then carefully extricated the body from the net before rolling him back into the water. As the body floated, he reached out and grabbed the mask, yanking it from around the man's neck. He rolled up his net, gathered his fish, then made the trek up the riverbank to his humble home where four generations lived.

He stopped behind a large tree and tied the mask to his face, then continued around the final bend in the path. His wife gasped and the children squealed in fear at the horrifying image he must have presented. He laughed and removed the mask.

"It's just me!"

His children rushed forward and hugged him, then he handed off the fish and his gear to them as he approached his wife, washing clothes.

"Where did you find that, Husband?"

He gave her a quick kiss. "In the river. I found it in my net." He didn't mention the body it had been attached to, as he was certain she would disapprove of what he had done.

She took it and held it up in the fading light, smiling. "It's beautiful."

He shrugged. "Only you could find beauty in something so grotesque."

She grinned at him. "Well, I married you, didn't I?"

He laughed and clutched at his heart. "Oh, how you wound me, woman."

She took the mask inside and placed it on a shelf in their living area. "I think it looks good there."

He agreed. "I'm going to wash up. Let me know when dinner is ready."

"I will."

He headed outside, the children having already brought out the wash bin and supplies, and as he went through his post-fishing ablutions, he thought of the man and his fine clothes, and the odd mask he had been wearing. It must have had some meaning, though what that was, he had no idea.

Certainly, it never occurred to him that by tradition, as the first man to wear the Mask of Succession after the king's death, that he was now king of Ayutthaya, and would remain so, unbeknownst to himself and the kingdom he by tradition ruled, until its collapse a mere nine years later, a collapse that forced his family to flee to more peaceful lands.

Until a deluge killed him and his family, wiping out their new home and village.

And burying the Mask of Succession with Ayutthaya's last king.

THE END

ACKNOWLEDGMENTS

This book was a lot of fun to write. I had the concept for the history, with two brothers feuding for the throne, and plotted the entire thing before doing a deep dive into the kingdom in question to plug the holes. What I found was actually shocking.

I had it uncannily close to the real history.

The only difference between what I wrote and what history recorded, is that the unworthy eldest son was tortured and killed by his father, who was by no means a nice guy. The rest matched remarkably well. I once again took history, and twisted it, this time only a half-turn, I suppose!

I get contacted by budding authors asking me how I write my action scenes. Many say they have no idea where to begin, how to describe things, etc. I find action scenes easy to write because I just picture them as a movie. It's like a reverse script. I picture it then write it, instead of writing it then filming it. When I write the scenes you read, I've already watched the movie.

Man, I think there are some good movies in this back catalog!

As usual, there are people to thank. My dad for all the research, Brent Richards for some weapons info, Ian Kennedy for some Molotov cocktail and boobytrap info (it's scary what this dude knows), and, as always, my wife, my daughter, my late mother who will always be an angel on my shoulder as I write, as well as my friends for their continued support, and my fantastic proofreading team!

To those who have not already done so, please visit my website at www.jrobertkennedy.com, then sign up for the Insider's Club to be notified of new book releases. Your email address will never be shared or sold.

Thank you once again for reading.

Made in United States
North Haven, CT
20 July 2023

39315966R00189